If you wer
killer or acce
choose?

Randy was faced with his worst living nightmare - his death - and given the choice of accepting the circumstances of his demise where he could find peace in the hereafter, or seek out the sordid truth with the assistance of the undead FBI.

It takes a lot to manage Limbo. It's a tough job and William has been running it for a very long time. The surprise came after Props brought Randy back to the other side, after stitching him back together he begins remembering things - details about his death that were impossible to know. That small spark of memories ignites a shining hope for him. But with all his knowledge and ambition, William still hasn't found a way to bring justice to his killer.

For some of the deceased, Limbo is home and a second chance to start over; giving them the chance to leave their colorful and sometimes treacherous pasts behind. For the living, some have found a secret entry into the perfect hiding place for organized crime - and they'll do whatever it takes to keep it that way.

The stakes will rise when the peace and bureaucracy in Limbo is threatened by a plot to get rid of the remaining evidence and the last two people who stand to bring an entire criminal organization to its knees! It'll take more than good sleuthing and innocent curiosity to bring justice to a place where some lives never end, and others can't begin.

With Randy still desiring escape from his death with the intent on starting over on the side of the living, the stakes will rise. Can he ever find true peace or will his selfish acts put everyone in Limbo in jeopardy?

Will a confrontational showdown through a cascade of events brings the realm of the living clashing with the land of the dead, unraveling a chain of dangerous events, bring their undead lives to a final curtain - once and for all?

Table of Contents

Title Page

Copyright Page

Introduction

Chapter 1

Chapter 2

Chapter 3

Chapter 4

Chapter 5

Chapter 6

Chapter 7

Chapter 8

Chapter 9

Chapter 10

Chapter 11

Chapter 12

Chapter 13

Chapter 14

Chapter 15

Chapter 16

Chapter 17

Chapter 18

Chapter 19

Chapter 20

Chapter 21
Chapter 22
Chapter 23
Chapter 24

Other Creative Works by Aralyn Kraft

Rules of Limbo

Better Luck Next Time
(Nothing But Time Series - Book 1)

Game Changer: MMORPG IRL

Export Compliance for Beginners

All books are available through Amazon.com

Rules of Limbo

Aralyn Kraft

This book is a work of fiction/fantasy. Any resemblance to actual persons, living or dead, names, characters, places and/or incidents is entirely coincidental and strictly from the author's imagination.

First edition.

ISBN: 9781983264030

Author Website: https://aralynblog.wordpress.com/

Available at:
Amazon.com, GoodReads.com, SmashWords.com

Cover created by Fiverr.com

© Copyright 2018 Tamatha Rawls (a.k.a. Aralyn Kraft)
All rights reserved.
No portion of this book may be reproduced in any form
without permission from the publisher, except as permitted
by U.S. copyright laws.

Rules of Limbo

Chapter 1

Rule No.1: The Dead are to remain dead.

Rule No.2: The Deaf can hear, don't talk too loud to them. The Blind can see, don't wave them down. The Mute can speak so don't let them ramble too much or they'll literally talk your head off.

Rule No.3: Refill the coffee maker. If you drink it, refill it.

Rule No. 4: Always close the door behind yourself.

It goes without saying, Rule No.3 applies whether you're dead or still living or just in a bizarre dream - like this one. Have a little courtesy!

Yet there are those who bend and even break that rule believing there is no consequence. Until they find a bunch of soggy coffee filters in their desk drawer, or worse, the coffee maker simply disappears one day with a ransom note left in its place demanding someone else foot the bill. Not that that's ever happened, but if it had, I would certainly not be the person to ask if I saw anything. There are simple rules we live by or society as we know it crumbles into chaos. And for some of us, coffee is the elixir that binds the universe together. A fact Dolores should have known before drinking the last cup and leaving the last few teaspoons left burn to the carafe, cracking it and destroying everyone's already miserable day.

And much like that infamous day for the staff, mine's been surreal. Like the in between stage of sleep where you think you're awake but still sleeping but might not be. The thing is, I can't tell if I'm still dreaming, or if whatever this is may be real. I'm not sure I wanna know. Everything was disjointed. I'm inclined to go with hallucinations brought on by leftovers and stale beer.

Somewhere in my exhausted foggy brain I wondered if hallucinations could actually hurt? Can they really be this painful? The memory of what I can only explain as a pulsing blue and white aura cocooned me; my eyes stinging and watering a lot at the intense brightness while everything was out of focus. A familiar dreaded sensation swept over me from head to toe of being wrapped tightly, mummified. Trying to stretch my arms and legs was near to impossible at first. I could barely sense my limbs as the muscles and tendons creaked like the wood flooring of an old house.

But getting the gumption to move and actually committing the act was a different story. Every joint snapped and popped, everything ached like the flu and every sound was waffling - either too muffled and soft to hear, as if I'd been swimming underwater, minus the chlorine up my nose, or banshee ear piercing scream level blaring in seconds.

Then came the all too familiar, distinct rich smells of coffee from almost everywhere around me, and some guy in a sharp tailored suit talking a mile a minute in my ear, leading me brusquely by my limp arm across some street named Cragston. My legs were as heavy as lead, so here's where I got the idea I'm dreaming because waking up with the blankets swaddled around our legs kinda feels like that. Like you're trapped and weighed down and feeling panicky when really we're simply tangled in our sleep. We've all done it. Right?

Anyway, here was this guy handing me a book about an inch thick, rambling with a polished and professional accent like he was a lawyer from New York or somewhere up East, chatting a mile a minute about seeing someone named Vanessa. If that wasn't weird enough to be unforgettable, since I haven't known anyone from the Bronx in ages, then the way he shook my hand briskly like a CEO then none too gently pushed me in the direction of a set of double glass doors definitely was. I think he said good luck before he abandoned me there. Going on pure instinct alone and still pretty confused, I didn't even ask, I just shuffled my zombie feet, one in front of the other inside. Now, I'm no stranger to the after effects of moderate-to-severe drinking after a night out with my friends but this was excessive and made me wonder if someone had slipped me something in my drink. There was no way I could still be this sluggish all over as if I'd overslept from a nasty hangover. Even my mouth didn't work right and felt like someone had stuffed it with cotton balls after knocking the crap outta my jaw. It's not a particularly pretty vision but hey, it's my dream, right? Here's hoping it's just a dream and I'm not hallucinating in some hospital from an overdose of whatever it was I ate in my fridge. Besides, my ears were beginning to ring clear up and so were my other faculties.

Here's where I thought it was weird, not that waking up feeling like a cross between a hangover and the flu is normal for me but, I tugged self-consciously at my collar and looked around the room. It was oddly familiar. Not the type of familiar you automatically recognize when you wake up from a weird detailed dream and go, "Oh, hey I must be in my bedroom," or self-realization that you must have sleep-drove on autopilot into the office today and wonder how many red lights and stop signs you accidentally missed.

Such remarkable similarity in details to the awake version of my office downtown, all the way down to the crappy green carpeting and old-fashioned walnut paneling. Announcing her presence by the clicking of her high heels as she walked, some barbie doll looking woman in a tight size ten or twelve yellow dress that looked like a throwback from the 1960's or 70's, scowled at the still revolving door behind me before clipping over and holding out her hand, offering to escort me to an office I think I remember seeing only a handful of times before - you know, when I'm awake. Sitting behind the desk she offered the chair in front and I sat obediently across, staring wide eyed, holding the book for no apparent reason, thrumming my fingers respectfully.

"I suppose the jerk simply dumped you off at the door and rushed away," she huffed aloud blowing a short disgruntled breath into her bangs. "You poor kid. Dump and run. Who does that?" Her voice sounded a bit like the guy who, according to her, dumped me here a few moments earlier but with a twinge of maybe New Jersey or Queens thrown in. It was hard to tell, but I pegged her as a cross between the Queens and Brooklyn type, like in the movies - a little nasally, enunciating the vowels more than necessary and with her looks, it fit.

Exasperated, she sighed shaking her head, grabbing a pen and opened a manila folder. "The effects you're feeling will pass soon enough: dry mouth, bloated all over, general fogginess, fatigue. Until then we'll just have to muddle through the orientation," she said nodding. I didn't want to stare but there was something odd about her face making her difficult to read. Normally you can tell what type of person is talking to you by their smile or frown, squinting eyes - movements. But that's what was missing. All those little quirks. If it hadn't been for the change of tones in her voice, I'd say she had a good shot at being a robot. A very good looking feminine robot. Which meant she was way out of my league, especially in a dream. "Okay, the paperwork is boring but a necessary evil formality so let's get right to it." Her voice resonated with that perkiness that comes from having been rich, pampered, or a high school queen. "Do you remember your name?" That's stupid, of course I know my name.

My inner voice cackled and huffed until I tried pulling my name from the place inside my brain that says, 'you are'. I blinked rapidly and tried harder shaking my head. "It's okay. It takes most newbies about a week to get oriented. Your name should come back to you in a day or two." Again I shook my head, confused, numbly agreeing this time. "Do you remember precisely what you were doing last?" This time I licked my chapped lips, thinking hard. These should have been easy, even in my sleep. How far under was I? I didn't remember drinking at any bars or taking any medications or smoking anything that'd put me out this far.

"Could've been home." That didn't sound right, "No - somewhere else." I'm usually out with one of the people from work. There was this girl, Gina? Tamara? Maybe we had drinks. No, wait- was I with the regulars at the bar? No, they haven't been around much lately. Reaching harder into my memories my brows pulled tight. A bead of sweat began forming at my hairline, threatening to spill and make a run straight for my eye. Was I sick at home or something? Oh wait! As inconceivable as it seems, I squirmed in the seat, at the mere suggestion forming, I'd probably worked late. "I, uh, might have been at my desk, I presume." The words formed through my speech impaired tongue but coughing a bit seemed to clear that up.

"You can't presume. You either know for a fact or you don't. Now, do you remember your last whereabouts?" Clicking the pen in her hand she waited impatiently, but something flickered in her eyes. Something vague that disappeared as soon as she realized I had been staring back.

"At my desk. Definitely at my desk. At work." The expression she'd given left as quick as it had slid into place. What if she's testing me or checking to see if I'm paying attention? I'm taking the moment as a hint. What else could it be? If I'm still at work, then maybe that's where I've fallen asleep. Maybe that's what the look means. She's in my dream to warn me I've dozed off on the job and about to get into serious trouble. Because I definitely don't remember leaving the office. Oh crap, I'm probably in the bathroom. Oh gods, I hope not! That means this is one of those off the wall dreams where my boss is about to walk inexplicably through the doors, open this stall, and carry on an awkward conversation about something inane he did golfing he was proud of or smoke a cigarette while just standing there - staring, judging me. I bet my pants are around my ankles, or worse, I'm about to find out I'm naked with nothing but my neck tie, socks and shoes on. I think I wanna throw up.

"Good," she said, clicking the pen again and scribbling her notes, bringing me out of my temporary distracting nightmarish thoughts. "Your file doesn't mention hobbies, sports, friends, family, wife," she paused inquisitively peering up, "girlfriend?" Again I shook my head negative. What? I had all those things. Didn't I? I mean there was what's her name and that guy at that place that time and...oh lord. "By the look on your face, you're probably still in shock. I suppose we should put this off for a day or two, until you remember more. Until then, we'll assign you a desk job, much the same thing you had been doing in your old routine. Maybe that'll help jar things a bit." Standing, I shook her hand and didn't know why I was thanking her but somehow I instinctively knew I needed to follow her and do as I was told. "This will be yours for now. Copier is in the corner, supplies in the cabinet there and I will remind you to please read the book you were given and pay special attention to Rule No.3. People can get mighty pissy about their caffeine."

As she turned to leave I finally found my voice, "Where am I?" Peering at me beneath perfectly curled blonde bangs a small sad smile played at the edges of her lips.

Sliding her pen behind her ear she replied, "Have you ever heard of a little place called Limbo? That special slice of death between here and there?" Expressionless I waited for the punchline, looking over my desk, watching her tap the files in her hands with exquisite manicured nails.

"Uh huh, right. Limbo-o-o," I drawled, adding a disbelieving courtesy nod. It was all I could do to keep from out right laughing. "And, why am I here?"

"Well, the best I can tell you is you died and sort of ended up in the Bureau's Awakening room." Her short blond hair barely moved as she spoke, accentuating her porcelain face. Maybe too much hairspray or something but it was a cute 1960's cross between Jackie O and Marilyn Monroe look on her where someone else might not be able to pull it off. "It was really something to see

Props work so fast on you. And let me tell you, they had the work order in hand before your body hit the slab. Somebody must have thought you were worth it."

I wasn't buying whatever story she was selling, "But why? Why here? Wherever here is." Uncomfortably, she shifted her gaze, thrumming her nails in a soft, quiet, rehearsed pattern across the tops of the files.

"When we die, we're sorted out into here and there, the ultimate places we end up. You, like some others, have no here or there. Most likely a glitch in your file. Until we get it sorted out and you accept the results, you're to remain in Limbo. Then we can send you on."

"You mean heaven and hell? I'm dead and in one of those two?" Blowing a harsh breath between my lips, I shook my head, "I knew I shouldn't have ate that old spaghetti. It tasted kinda funny," I chuckled, smacking my lips, rubbing my stomach. "This dream is so weird. Okay, let's say I believe you - which I don't. I'm stuck in hell until you can send me back to my bedroom and I wake up on the floor of my apartment with a hangover and stomach ache. Man, I hope I'm not out of antacids."

"No silly, I mean here and there. Heaven and Hell are concepts; imagination if you will. An individual's need to have labels for their final destinations. No, what I'm talking about is a place you reside between those two places." Screwing up my face I knew I looked like I'd just eaten a piece of squid that'd been laying in the sun too long and marinated in lemon juice then deep fried in tobacco and stale tempera. Eww! "On occasion, people die of horrendous deaths, mysteries, or even, dare I say, boredom. In those cases, the Bureau has no idea what to do with them until their case is investigated and given a formal determination." At least she looked like she took pity. "Don't worry. It'll all come together for you. For now, try to do your best, fit in, and don't be too late for work."

"Bed?" Great, I was monosyllabic, even in my dream. I have to remember to work on that when I get up. That, and clean out the fridge.

"Oh, my!" She exclaimed laughing, "I'm a space case, aren't I?" Reaching into her front pocket of her dress, she pulled out a key and a card. "Here's your backup key to the apartment and a card to use when you need anything. As for the key, it'll work on all kinds of doors, but you'll have time for that later. The address is already programmed inside the card. The map appears when you ask the card to show you where to go. Just follow it and you'll be fine." Waving she abruptly turned, her shoes tapping away in high heels. Maybe she was in a hurry to follow up on another case or start another tour of, what'd she call it, Limbo?

By habit, I reached to adjust my glasses and found they weren't there, but I could see fine. Another tick which means I'm still in some dream state. I hate my glasses; hate I have had to wear them all my life. But so as long as I'm here, and I have near perfect vision, a place to work and sleep, I might as well enjoy the trippy ride.

Chapter 2

I'd been at 'work' for nearly five hours churning out much the same pink, yellow, and white triplicates of budget and financial file summaries as I do when I'm awake. Which just goes to show, either I'm so good at my job I can do it in my sleep, or it's so banal no one else wants to do it. At least in my awake job I have a computer and a couple of monitors, but this is worse than archaic, it's manual. As in pencil whipping numbers without a calculator into a paper ledger. Paper! I'm in worse shape than I thought. I remember reading about this process in college but I've never actually done it. My brain is making this harder than it should be.

Which leads me to my internal dialog. Why am I doing my waking job in my sleep when I should be dreaming something cool? Like white water rafting? Even though I'm scared to death of fast moving deep water. Or I could be skydiving with a gorgeous chick; or not. Got this phobia about unsecured heights and meeting new people , especially beautiful ones. Okay, I'm over analyzing this. If I concentrate on being at the beach on a sunny day, the wind tugging my hair, the call of never ending pina coladas magically appears in my hands, and stop being so fussy, maybe I can salvage this nightmare.

Then again, I keep getting these disjointed scary images in my head of bits and pieces of jagged debris and papers flying everywhere. I know it's just a dream, but it feels so - real. As in scary real. Real enough to make my hands shake and my palms sweat, my heart race and the back of my neck prickle. And well, to be honest, there's also this sort of half-paranoia half-reality check my subconscious likes to do in my sleep when I can't wrap my head around something when I'm awake. I call it W.O.A.L., pronounced wall, like the mental ones we build to protect ourselves from shit like this, but still, wrong on-all-levels.

For instance, right now it seems as though a keen set of eyes are on me, watching my every move. Yet I don't see anyone, anywhere. When I'm in my awake office, I get the same sensation of being scrutinized by what's his name, my jerk supervisor. Okay, that's different. The guy I can't stand who sends me on ridiculous errands all the time. The vulture of an excuse for a human being who stands right there in that very hallway; always looking at his watch impatiently. Why can't I remember his name? Okay, not that it really matters. The fact he's disappeared in my fake work dream world and I can't remember his name is a major bonus not to be over thought. But theses odd things keep trickling a little at a time into my brain while I'm quietly paper shuffling and pencil pushing. A dream within a dream? Will I need a therapist when I wake up? Maybe. But I'm definitely cleaning out the fridge soon.

So, instead of sticking my toes in luxuriously warm soft white sandy beaches and having cool turquoise ocean spray tickling my nose, I somehow managed to stick myself with pink papers and yellow carbon copies who remain firmly stacked in the in-box on the corner of my apologetically dull desk. The far wall, where what's his name usually paces, holds a small coffee table covered in those little packets of sugars and creamers, and a water cooler standing alongside with piles of boxes nearly as high as the ceiling. The worst part is somehow knowing all those boxes are for me.

But a job's a job whether asleep or awake, so blue is most important and gets tackled first. Plus, who knows, maybe the blues are jokes or riddles or something cartoonish here. Nothing. Damn. There isn't any so triplicate. Pinks come with yellow carbon copies and white gets signed and sent to management or finance. Repetitive and boring as hell but since I don't know where either one is, just go on to the daily budgets. But as my fingertips slide across each form they begin tremble lightly. Laying the first pages on the desk I scanned, reading fast through all the redundant: this box is the amount due, that box is the amount paid, and the summary box at the bottom that's supposed to be the sum of everything added and subtracted within the form. Blah, blah, blah. Only an hour of this and my eyes wanted to cross all on their own. My hands still shook a little but enough to wonder if I'd had anything to eat. I'm guessing my stomach was awake and gurgling and belly aching for something other than traumatizing leftovers. It could account for the aching in my head and the trembling.

And wouldn't you know, as soon as I stood up to bring myself out of this stupid dream and eat for real, people deliberately walked by with folders in their hands and the blank look everyone gets when they have something on their mind they're in the middle of and don't want to lose that train of thought.

Speaking of…

don't you just hate when you're in the middle of nothing more than a possible thought of going to get sustenance, when and an odd blue piece of paper suddenly appears in your inbox? I Never saw who placed the paper but when I looked around, the office had cleared out of people. Turning my attention to it, I lifted the corner halfheartedly; after all, the memo was a different color and looked important. But I had to wonder if something really is urgent why give it to me? I mean, I'm the new guy and all. Or am I? Dreams can be so weird. Who do these people think I am? This is my mental state of unconsciousness and I really don't feel like analyzing myself! What do they expect me to do? Or maybe this part of the dream is what I've been waiting to happen in real life - the opportunity to be noticed. To do something more with my life other than shuffle papers and balance ledgers. Someone was finally giving me a chance to be more than a budget clerk. *Better not blow it.*

Curiosity bubbled at my fingertips as I read the request:

Props Dept. low on Supplies. Attend immediately!

As I folded the paper in half more words rose beneath my fingertips, as if by, dare I say magic. But then again, they could have simply been written there the whole time and I didn't notice it:

Now newbie!

For a brief moment I tentatively held the paper between my fingers, gently tugging at the middle, getting ready to tear it in half when another message appeared:

Don't make me come down there. Now!

"Fine," I huffed rolling my eyes. Leaving my desk I pulled out the key card and spoke to it, feeling stupid all the while. "Take me to…um, Props." When the little silver and copper piece of plastic did nothing but stare back at me from an empty white surface, I sighed trying not to throw it across the room. Slumping my shoulders I tried in disgust again, "Okay, let's try this. Where is Props?" This time the copper ran up and around making an outline of what looked like the street I crossed earlier and a small town surrounding it. The line continued to draw until it came to a square in the upper left-hand corner and blinked, of all things. As if to say, "This is your destination. Can you get there now?"

Following the slightly ambiguous directions on the card, I left the office, heading up the street called Cragston and made a left on Shirley Avenue. The line on the card continued to shine copper as long as I stayed on track. If I strayed, even a little, it hummed in my hand until I corrected my course. So much for sightseeing.

What felt like a hundred city blocks later became a tiny storefront where the sign read: Artemis, Mortimer, and Flo's Props Department.

Inside as I closed the door, the chimes above rang, alerting the extremely large, dank space I had arrived. From the rafters through the dim lighting cast by the dirty windows, fell a constant silent snow of dust, adhering to everything it touched. Everywhere were stacks of wooden crates of all sizes, pallets of stacked boxes, and thirty gallon sealed containers, all coated in the stuff.

In seconds three figures in overalls and loose-fitting shirts with latex gloves appeared through a door to my right I had not seen earlier. Eagerly they removed their gloves snapping their fingers and practically hopping on their toes as they came closer. Each wore a stitched name tag identifying their owners as Art, Morty, and Flo; I presumed they were the owners.

The one labeled Art pointed at me, giggling, shaking his finger wildly. "Told ya we had company. I can hear a mile away."

Rolling his eyes, the one known as Morty huffed, "Yeah we know. And for the millionth time, I still say it was a mistake fixing your ears." Art waved away at him as if he were an annoying fly buzzing around.

Pocketing my card I wanted to introduce myself but

since it was just a dream I chilled my initial anxiety. I mean, really, who remembers their name in a dream anyway and second, this one was getting interesting.

"Nice place you got here. What's with all the dust?" I asked looking down the aisle in front of me.

"Uhh, it's not all dust. Try not to inhale the larger flakes for now," Arty smirked, scrunching his face as if he'd smelled something awful while handing me a mask resembling one of those paper thin antivirus masks you get at the doctor's office.

"Ohh kay. So, what's with the name tags?" I pointed to their chests as they peered down at themselves.

"Oh," Flo snorted with a giggle, "some of us have a tough time remembering certain li'l things, you know, like my name. So the Bureau lets us carry notes with us. That way we can find our way around and talk to one another and introduce ourselves to newcomers like yourself."

"Newcomers," I repeated blandly. "Word gets around fast in la-la land."

"We have a hand or two with everyone who comes through here--literally. At some point," the one tagged Morty chuckled, shrugging modestly, "you literally get familiar with everyone inside and out."

"I'm sure he don't wanna hear about our patchwork jobs," the ginger with a kind face grinned, patting Morty on the shoulder. Her red hair reached the middle of her back with gracefully aged white patches making her look a little calico. The gentle waves of her hair matched the few laugh lines around her soft but keen eyes. She reminded me of one of the adoption family's aunt I once met. Kind, sweet and I bet she knows a lot more than she leads on. "That's Art, don't get him started on a story, he'll likely talk yer ears off. This here's Morty," she said as the gentlemen shook my hand in turn, "and I'm Flo."

"And Flo would be short for what, Florence?" I asked. Bobbing her head side to side with a vivacious smile she answered.

"Nah I couldn't remember my name when I got here and when they asked me what I'd like to be called, I said I'd go with the flow. They shortened it to F-l-o. Kinda cute huh."

"Where ya from?" Art asked, his Brooklyn accent as thick as the dust in the room.

"Uhm, not sure. I'll have to get back to you on that."

"Ah, a lotta folks take a bit to get oriented. That's fer sure," Arty smiled, squinting as he looked the aisle over behind them. The faint sound of boxes shifting in the distance alerting his senses. When the moment passed, he shrugged and returned his attention to me. I gotta say, Irish is the best accent to mix with Brooklyn. It gives this kind of don't mess with me or I'll mess with you not so nicely air.

"So, the boss sent you. How long ya been here sweetie?" Flo asked, her accent branding her a southerner.

"Around five hours," I replied as Morty's features crinkled, scrutinizing me closer.

"They don't send newbies on errands that fast. You must be special. You sure you don't remember where you're from?" Morty asked. As I stood there hearing his question, it came to me.

"Somewhere in Idaho. Boise, I think."

"Told ya," Flo said haughty, putting her hands to her hips. "Knew this one was different."

As they carried on the conversation in ordinary questions and strange looks for answers, it occurred to me - my dream was my subconscious who may be coming down with a cold or flu. I was obviously delusional with a fever and still asleep. Mental note - check and recheck on when I'm going to clean out the fridge. If I'm going to be sick, I want my mind to take me somewhere nice, like the Bahamas or the Grecian Islands.

Waving off the rest of the questions politely I walked around the stacked room leaving deep imprints of my shoes in the thick settling dust. Heading toward the middle of the back of the odd place, a piles of boxes leaned one on top of another against a large crate. The area I saw Morty listen towards earlier intrigued me. Below, as I began trying to push the heavy boxes back into place I noticed footprints had led to and from a door at the back of the building to that spot, leading along the edge toward the front of the building. The door at the back seemed old and mildly warped with chipped paint being its main feature.

"I'll get that," Morty's voice startled me as I turned, his feet now smearing the extra set of prints. "Don't need to trouble yourself with our messes." Pushing the boxes hard with his shoulder, he shoved them into place quickly and neatly. "Remind me to give you a tour of the place sometime," he said as I heard a soft click a few aisles back. Leaning in close enough to whisper, he escorted me toward the front door, "You're always welcome here, kid. Day or night don't matter. You always got a place. Understand?" Patting my back we made our way back to where Flo stood wringing her hands and Art paced impatiently in a four foot strip. As Morty opened the front door, I took that as my polite queue to leave.

"I'll see what I can do," I said as I tipped my hand waving goodbye and found it humorous when I stepped outside. Their names were part of an embalming process, the cosmetic part, I think. I remember watching the documentary something like a week ago. Maybe it messed with my subconscious more than I thought. I'll blame that for now.

Somewhere between the time I left to investigate the sound of the shifting boxes and when Morty came to stop me from finding whatever it was I wasn't suppose to find, the information came out that they were workers but not proprietors of the shop. Apparently, as Flo had explained, the mortuary around here is actually called the Props Department. Its function is similar to a mortician who dresses up the deceased for viewing so the living don't freak out. Around here though, their job is much more difficult; they literally stitch people back together the best they can and apply a makeup base to make them more presentable. I took that as a way of politely saying, 'we fix you and dress you up so you can live with yourself.' That, and they bring you back to life somehow. I didn't ask; I didn't want to know.

My imagination did not want to go to the unhappy place of vivid drama so I simply nodded politely as Morty and Art argued and finally got around to explaining their dilemma. They'd had their order of putty, salts and everything else for quite some time but the order hadn't been fulfilled. If I hadn't left when I did, there's no telling how long they would've talked. Besides, no one seems to know how to follow up on these little things but I suppose if my subconscious is really riled about this kind of stuff in the real world, at least maybe I can sort them out and be happy with the results in this one.

Eyeing the card in my hand I twirled it between my fingers a few times and saw both sides were empty. Uncomfortable with the idea I was literally talking to an inanimate object, I coughed politely and spoke to it again,

"Find the Prop's order." Again the surfaces were blank. Deflated from guessing, I tried one last time, "Take me to the Prop's order." This time the copper glowed and shot off down the street and stopped seven stores down. "Really?" I said, growing flustered. And as I approached the place on the map, the copper outline disappeared. "They couldn't just walk over here and get this?" Shaking my head in disbelief, I pocketed the card and opened the door to an incredible warehouse. It's all I could do not to be overly impressed and want to roller skate around the place.

Aisle upon aisle stood cartons and crates stacked neatly halfway to three-quarters of the way to the ceiling for as far as the eyes could see in any direction. Overhead, compact fluorescent lights occasionally flickered and hummed setting a B rated horror film type scene. I knew if I were in trouble, yelling in that size of a place would make no difference. But it was a dream and you can do anything, including perform miracles and scream without incident in them.

"Hello?" my voice echoed only a few feet away, drowned by the buzzing of the few lights left in the ballasts that had not been blown and dampened by the sheer size of the and volume of the containers stacked neatly. "Is anyone here?" I have to admit, I've never had a creepier moment awake or otherwise then walking through a place that dwarfed me in size and made me feel like a villain with a burned face and long claws was going to suddenly jump out and tear me into shredded brisket any second.

The hair on the back of my neck stood, giving me goosebumps I subconsciously rubbed. Cracking my knuckles out of a nervous habit, I didn't want to appear as though I didn't know what I was doing so I pocketed my hands in the back of my jeans and browsed around. "I've come to see about Prop's order. Anyone here?" At the far end, the lights began to turn off, one set at a time, one row at a time. As the darkness crept toward where I stood, I backed up involuntarily. The hair on the nape of my neck tingles at the thought of being alone in the dark in this place; and made my stomach want to roll - or was it because I wasn't alone. "Is someone there?" my voice squeaked. In the dim edges of the darkness came a shadow stepping out around one of the large pallets. The light on the front of the helmet coming on as the rest of the surrounding lights expired. "I've come for Prop's stuff; if you'll just show me where it's at, I'll take it over to them." Wordless, he moved almost robotic toward me. I never liked horror and suspense movies, they give me the willies and this was fairly reminiscent of that. "Just point the way and I'll not bother you." Still backing my way toward the exit the lights went out, enveloping us all except for the hat that seemed to dim where we stood.

Chapter 3

The rusted bay door creaked loud enough to wake the dead; slamming to the concrete floor as it slipped from my grip. From the outside the building had appeared fragile, small and to be in disrepair like most of the other brick and mortar counterparts lining the streets. Color me surprised when I peered up and down inside the place. Tall enough to stack three giraffes on top of each other and amazingly complex maze of crates lines row upon row of the nearly five story building; which might not have been so implausible had I not watched science fiction shows most of my life. Things can seem small on the outside and deceptively bigger on the inside, especially if you're standing at one end watching batches of lights turn off and on in a sequel pattern.

"Hello?" I called out. The sound barely echoed falling as flat as the concrete surface. Clearing my throat, I announced again, raising my voice with more authority, "Hello! Anybody here?"

Overhead as the lights went out, one by one, my breath blew between my pursed lips that I hadn't realized I'd been holding. The batches had been replaced by a floating dot at head level, slowly becoming a bouncing ball of light, carrying beneath it footsteps shuffling at a quick pace.

"Got a packing list?" a gruff older male voice spoke next to a tidy stack of boxes nearby, startling me.

"No," I replied a little more timid than usual. "They didn't tell me I needed one." More shuffling moved away as his voice followed, resonating.

"Amateurs," he gruffed as I heard a click and an engine start by the end of the aisle. The grumbling mechanism turned the corner and headed my way. Carrying with it the strange little man who brought the forklift to a stop only a few feet away. It had been augmented with what looked like an old recliner and some sort of well used short rubber rails added to the sides. Hopping down, he walked stiffly past me with intent in his steps.

"So, how big is this place?" I asked, having to job to keep up with his pace. For an old guy, he sure moves with hamster feet.

"Plenty big." Turning down another aisle he halted abruptly and climbed into a cage on wheels. I couldn't be sure, but it might have started out as another forklift; but with all the changes to it, you really were unable tell anymore. The safety horn and back up beeper sounded as he turned the machine around and looked at a clipboard hanging from the side. "Best you come with me," he grunted, indicating I should get on and hold on. With his driving, it was more like hold on for your life.

Grumbling under his voice, he maneuvered the machine up and down aisles with haste, pausing just long enough to read something marked on the sides of pallets then take off at high speed again. We stopped a moment later where I jumped down to safety from the side of his perch and waited for him to manage pulling an entire stack, three quarters high to the ceiling, skillfully with the tines of the machine.

"What is this place?" I asked, trying to be nosey and polite.

"Warehouse," the sullen man with frizzy white hair answered, but didn't comment further.

"So, what's in all these boxes?" I asked.

Glaring from beneath his hat, the little man shook his head, "Stuff." When he had the items turned around, we headed back to where I'd entered the door, and the bay beside it creaked open automatically.

Peering around expectantly, the odd fellow looked at me questioningly, "Where we going?"

"Props," I said knowingly. He just gave me a shrug and waited.

"Where's that?" Pulling the card from my pocket I asked where Props was and he followed the directions on my card; letting me ride on the side the two blocks instead of walking.

36

After depositing the crates in the corner of Prop's warehouse, I called out to let them know I was there and the strange little man left quickly without a word. Flo and Arty arrived looking pleased and patted me on the back for a job well done, smiling genuinely. I think, in all my life, I've never actually felt real pride until then. It wasn't anything awesome, or fantastic, or a world saving event; I just got their order and brought it to them - simple. But maybe somewhere in my dream state, I wanted the adulation, the admiration of others, my peers to recognize my talents for what they were. Maybe it was something I was missing in the waking world. Maybe I was just a little lonely, and maybe I was overthinking things.

I really don't like dreams; especially when I can't control them and had no idea where this one was taking me. I also don't like analyzing them and there's just no simple way to figure out what my subconscious was saying until this one's over. So being true to my not so curious nature, I headed back to my imaginary desk, where my imaginary job was waiting for me.

As some good moments must come with the bad, so was the moment I walked in the door at work and behold, Vanessa was waiting for me, tapping her foot, still holding a stack of files.

"Just where have you been? We've been looking everywhere." Worry or consternation? With her you never know. Her features are almost always perfect and barely move; except for the smile and blinking eyes.

"We?" I asked. For a moment I thought she was talking about the imperial we, you know as in one's self; but then the suit who had escorted me across the street earlier in the day came out of a room down a hall that I hadn't noticed before. Taking a place beside her, they seemed barely aware of each other's presence; until they spoke.

"We were afraid you'd gotten lost or something," he smirked. It's not like I'm a great judge of character or anything but the way he grinned made me shrink inward like a tuna swimming next to a great white shark, waiting to be eaten. "Where'd you go off to?"

Oh how the snarky side of me wanted to tell him, 'I was on business for the big boss and it's no business of yours,' but what came out was more truthful, after a gulp of air to regain composure under that icy glare. "I received an important note that told me to go run an errand; so I did."

"What sort of note?" he asked dubiously, crossing his arms over his chest.

"There," I said, pointing to the blue note I'd left in plain sight on my desk. After picking it up and looking it over thoroughly, he huffed and grinned, just like my old supervisor used to do when he didn't quite believe me, or his own eyes. In the blink of an eye, his posture changed to a more relaxed pose; even his expression went from disbelieving to contemplation.

"Just let us know in the future if you intend to go off again. We'd hate to lose track of you so soon after arriving here." Folding the note, he pocketed it and gave me one of those fake smiles used car salesmen give when they know they've snookered you.

"It's blue," Vanessa leaned with a whisper, as he paused next to her.

"I know," he responded in the same conspiratorial whisper. After a questioning glare and quick non-verbal exchange, the man left Vanessa to pick up where she left off. Setting her jaw firmly, she knew she'd been dismissed. Whatever their working relationship is has got to be a culmination of leftovers from the fridge and some bad weed or something. I can't even imagine what part of my waking existence this represents.

"That must have been exciting," she finally said, on a perkier note. Even with little to no facial expressions, I could see in her eyes she wasn't as okay with her situation as she lead on. Maybe she didn't like being a supervisor or something. Who knows? I just didn't want to get involved in another office soap opera drama, especially in my sleep.

"It was fine." Even though I acted nonchalantly and shrugged it off, I knew I was trying to hide something from her. I have no idea why. I just followed my instincts that said not to trust some people here; even if it was a weird rendition of the waking world, I knew when to keep my mouth shut.

"You must be exhausted. I can walk you to your apartment if you want." She offered, but for some reason I didn't feel like being in her company; or in this dream anymore. All I wanted was to wake up for real in my own comfy bed, in my little cold apartment, with a little space heater and order some fresh takeout.

"I got this," I said in the most polite way I could without sounding like a brush off; but that's what it essentially was, a push in her direction.

I think she was looking forward to some company but I wasn't looking forward to hers. I guess she sensed that because she turned slowly, walking away, "Okay then. I'll see you in the morning. If you need anything, just ask the card for my phone number. It'll call me." It was the second time today I'd been left completely alone with nothing special to do and no one to hold me accountable. Part of me felt like crap treating her like that but part of me just wants to be alone right now. Besides, it's hard to believe I'm that way to people when I'm awake. I'm a sweet, lovable, cuddly, teddy bear kinda guy who happens to eat alone in a dinky apartment almost every night. But I have friends I socialize with every weekend and six out of ten times they invite me out and I end up sitting at some club or bar, waiting half the night for them to arrive. The other half of the night I go home alone to that dinky, cold, mildew crusted place I call home.

This isn't looking so good for me.

As I picked up the book I was supposed to read and thumbed through the pages, it looked daunting, like a government manual and a lot to take in. So I planned to make it a night of take-out dinner, soda-pop, and reading; then I remembered, it's a dream and I have no money on me, real or imaginary. Why not go big?

"Steak and potatoes it is."

Chapter 4

As far as apartments go, it wasn't bad. It was almost identical to my own real one. My imagination had most of the details right except for the missing chipped paint on the walls and the marred sparse third-hand furniture. No. This place was better. A fresh coat of paint and mostly the same style, just newer and a slightly different color than what I remembered. Maybe I need to address some of that when I wake up? I admit, the place could use a little less obvious neglect on my part and definitely less deterioration on the part of the landlord. Maybe if I did a little more to spruce up the place he'd take a bit off the rent? Or, maybe I should pay the rent that's overdue and not bother with the paint? Decisions, decisions, decisions.

The apartment had only taken a few moments to walk to, and I'd passed several people I've never seen before in the halls. As I slid the keycard into the door lock, it beeped and lit a green dot above the slot. A neighbor a few doors down smiled and yelled, "Welcome home," waving as I entered my new old establishment. Laying my key in the glass bowl by the door, I kicked off my shoes and slid them beneath the console table holding the bowl. Shuffling around the room it seemed everything was in place and out of place at the same time. It had that 'look' of mine but not the 'feel'. It is most definitely better. Cleaner. It's missing the dirty clothes scattered and hanging off the back of the furniture and piles of empty pizza and takeout boxes stacked in the far corner. Missing, also, is the few pieces of plastic ware I own chucked into the sink to be washed at some later point in time; and the roaches and mice who keep me company because, let's face it - I'm a slob.

It's just better not to overthink these things. "She said it was a card, a map, even a phone book. Wonder what else it can do?" Pulling the card from my pocket and plopping onto the couch, I grinned shaking my head, "Gotta get one of these when I wake up. Okay, I want to order a steak - medium, with a baked potato and vanilla milkshake to be delivered to my apartment. No pizza for me tonight!" Surprised wasn't the word. Stunned wasn't even close. Not sure what to expect, I turned it over in my hand and saw an icon of a cow appear with the word medium above it. Next to it appeared another icon of a milkshake and baked potato while beneath a timer began counting down from 31:18.

"Some dream! I can't just have it ready, it has to be made and delivered. Figures." Huffing a deflated sigh I leaned my head back against the cushions, I closing my eyes against the lighting. Gentle pulsing sensations across my forehead and through my chest began creeping up and down my face and arms. The sensation didn't tingle, at first, but the longer I had my eyes closed, the stronger the pulses became.

In moments, the pulsing was in rhythm with my heartbeat, pounding through my entire body; sending signals along nerves and leaving them hot. My mouth was open and huffing for air, leaving the back of my throat dry. Flashes of red lights danced pushing and pulling under my eyelids. Indistinguishable ghostly squawks, like you'd hear in those horror movies where one of the expendable characters is about to be disposed of - screamed a high pitched siren, splitting in my skull; followed by insistent pounding around me. A dreaded sensation of falling uncontrollably shook me all over, and at the last second my body spasmed, falling for real onto the unforgiving carpeted floor in a swift knee-jerk reaction. Blinking hard and fast, my hands went to my eyes, rubbing them as I heard the pounding again. The card fell from my grip next to me, the countdown timer reading 00:00.

"Just a sec," my voice cracked. Reaching behind me I leveraged myself up with the aid of the couch, my knees aching from the rude awakening. Rubbing them I stumbled to the door, opening it with a meager effort.

"Steak, potato, shake. Enjoy!" The elderly Asian lady smiled. Giving me a quick cursory once over, she handed the paper bag and large styrofoam cup through the opening and waved as I took them and closed the door.

"Crap, I really should'a tipped her. Oh yeah, no money. Why don't I have money? Hell, I could have tipped her a couple a million, watched her light up light Christmas lights. Maybe she'd say, 'Oh thank you. You saved me from my terrible slumlord. Now I can pay the rent and buy the building and free everyone from his horrible clutches.' For that matter why the hell do I hurt? I shouldn't feel it, right? It's only a dream." Ambling toward the couch, I laid the bag at one end and crumbled into the cushions at the other end, sipping on the refreshing vanilla dessert. The shaking subsided but the idea of a mental breakdown inside of a dream was becoming a little scary. "And I'm talking to myself. Not a good sign," I said, rubbing at the soreness that shouldn't be in my knees.

Picking up the book, I adjusted and rolled my shoulders back against the seat wondering if I really was trying to solve my day problems in my sleep? Even if I had been the richest person on the planet, I don't think I would have tipped anyone a few extra million dollars let alone over the standard fifteen percent. I barely tip when I'm awake on what I make in a week. "Let's see what all the fuss is about." Cracking open the book to the middle, the first verse stared at me as blankly as I stared back at it. The words literally shook and jumped as I tried to concentrate. Yawning big, I stretched and tried again. This time I just couldn't comprehend anything I read and re-read, whether words or sentences over and over. "Nope. Not happening tonight." Putting the book aside, I let my mind wander back to earlier when I fell to the floor. "What the Hell happened?" Mulling the absurdity of the thought, I settled on dinner and sleep as my alternative plans. This will all be gone in the morning.

If dinner went a little too quick devouring the steak, then sleep also came way too fast in a bed that looked more comfy than my own. But as soon as my eyes closed those damn dancing lights came back. Along with waking every hour nearly on the hour from scary images popping brightly in my head of people flying through the air, glass bursting in every direction, bright lights of hospital ER, needles and loud voices. How was I suppose to wake up from this awful state unless I could get to sleep again, or still? Worse, what if I'm asleep at my desk at work? Could that be it? I remember going in but I don't remember leaving. Maybe someone's trying to prank me in my sleep and my subconscious is trying to warn me to wake up. They better leave my pen stash alone - that's all I'm saying. On top of the wrecking ball of a nightmare I'm having the last thing I need is to wake up with a marker pen mustache, or worse things, written on my face.

With the rising of the sun came a new day, way too early for some of us. In between the fitful tossing and turning from more of those vivid terrifying dreams, also came my not so sunny disposition from a lack of caffeine. Rolling exhausted to my feet, I stumbled to the nearest mirror in the bathroom. Feeling my face in a panic, I stared at my reflection, but the face looking back at me seemed - I dunno, different somehow. My hair was still cockatiel in nature, going every which way and straight up in the middle after sleeping on it; and though my face was a little pale, it was, in fact, permanent marker free. And while my hands explored the stubbled jaw working back and forth, I couldn't help but feel like I'd been kicked in the head or in a bar fight recently only without the contusions and abrasions that naturally go with me getting my ass kicked. No, something seemed off kilter - but then again, it could just be flu, or any number of things growing mold and fungus around the apartment. Fine. Mental note: clean apartment as soon as I wake up. Take out trash, clean out the fridge, wipe down walls, do laundry; or maybe just clean a few dishes. Okay, let's not be hasty and go overboard with the whole cleaning thing. Just go to the store and get a few paper plates and disposable cutlery, maybe take out some trash.

After a shower and dressing in yesterday's clothes and a cup of hot coffee, going to an office and working the same demeaning, useless, thankless job again seemed even more insignificant. But being stuck in a world created by my imagination, however, deemed a certain amount of exploration - so for once, I played hooky.

Eyeing the card laying in the bowl, I listened to that inner voice that said if I leave it here, for some weird, stupid reason, I'll find a use for it and not have it on me - like getting lost in my own world or something bat crazy shit like that. Pocketing my card, the handle to the front door turned too quickly in my grasp. The guy on the other side yelped as it pulled free of his grip and left me startled.

"Oh, hey there!" The medium built man with short mousy hair and a thin mustache cheerfully greeted me. "I was told to make sure you made it in on time; so, here I am." Perky. Why perky first thing in the morning? Why couldn't he have just shown up, waited politely for me outside, then ambushed me with the bad news like a normal person?

"Sorry, no can do," I said, nudging him from my doorway. "Got places to go, things to do — stuff." As the door clicked shut and locked behind me, his brows came together while still forcing a smile.

"But, I was told to come get you." I had to hand it to him, he was a company yes man and probably always did what he was told. The thin blue and yellow plaid button-up shirt said Henry in darker stitching. As he fidgeted, I looked up and down the empty hall.

"Look, Henry, I don't know how else to put it - this is my dream, my world, and my time. I'm going sightseeing. You can either come with, go back and tell them I'm not coming in, or go do something fun you want to do. Your choice."

"How'd you know my name?" he asked, surveying me with wild jumpy eyes.

Pointing to his chest I said, "It's printed on your shirt; right there." As he glanced down, the expression of bewilderment warred with disappointment and hope; thrown in with a little dash of excitement and viola! We have our thoroughly confused winner for the day.

Snapping his fingers in time to a melody no one heard and nodding, he looked up, "Oh, that was clever. They were right about you." Then he seemed to be waiting for something, or for me to say or do another marvelous trick. It was starting to get annoying.

"You know you don't have to babysit me. I'm a big boy and so are you." For an instant, by the clenching and unclenching of his fists, I prepared to duck the inevitable punch that was surely coming my way. Putting my hands up in front of me as an instinctive and quite useless shield, I muttered, "Let's just think about this."

Henry replied, blinking hard and fast as though he were trying to make up his mind. "Okay. I'll go - somewhere." Folding his hands across his chest nervously, he rocked on his heels. "Never been past the Station. What do you think?"

Lowering my hands, Henry made a sour expression watching them, "I think as long as I'm in one piece unmarked, that it would be an excellent suggestion." Sliding his arms to cross his chest, he stood there, acting like I'd just spoken a dialect from another world. At this point, I was willing to be a nice alien spaceship was going to be parked outside with nice little green men who happen to have a one-size-fits all straight jacket for me. And why not? This dream couldn't possibly get any weirder than that.

It seemed Henry was also a little slow at times to catch on, but when he did, I couldn't help but feel responsible, "Why would you think -?" There it was, the little innocent kid next door with teary puppy dog eyes look. I really do suck at reading people; people in a world my sleep conscious made.

"Nothing." I said, clearing my throat. "Just a little miscommunication on my part." It wasn't in my nature to take care of other people. Hell, it's not in my nature or best interest to take care of myself, but I found myself asking anyway, "Don't you have a card?" Not really caring or wanting to pry, but it did seem like if one of my figments of imagination were going to be here, they might as well have one too. I wouldn't want to have imaginary people getting lost in a world I created. That would just be irresponsible.

Fidgeting with the edge of his shirt, he shifted his gaze, uncertain of his whereabouts, "Yeah. But I only use it to run the errands I'm told to."

"How long you been here?" My subconscious just wouldn't shut up. Here I was trying to go have a beautiful day and it was trying to solve other people's problems.

"Oh, I dunno, a while or so." Henry stared at the wall, the ceiling, looked down the hall and up at the lights, anywhere but at me. For a second I wondered if I remembered to brush my teeth or put on deodorant until he leaned against the wall. "I can't do like you. I can't just go out places."

"You're not a prisoner. I wouldn't do that to my loyal subjects. Do what you will. Go where you want. No one's stopping you but you." Oh, that sounded rich coming from the guy who spends his nights curled up on the couch alone watching tv reruns and eating stale leftovers. Advice giver -- I'm not, but for some reason today, I was.
"Where would I go?"

"Somewhere other than the front of my apartment." It was meant to sound hopeful and a little pushy but by the glassy-eyed look, I had to wonder if I came across cantankerous because it sounded rude to me. And if my inner ear was hearing it, my mouth was probably saying it. "Look, I'm heading out. Nice meeting you. Maybe we'll bump into each other again sometime." The stairs raced beneath my swift moving feet, trying to get out the lobby door before someone else either found me or he decided to follow me. "Crap, the key." Well, as long as I had the card I was fine. That's what my brain was telling me. Everything was fine and would be fine. I felt fine. A person couldn't ask for a more fine day. Sunny blue skies, warm temperatures with a light breeze, and not a soul in sight. So if everything was fine why was my skin trying to crawl and this nagging sensation won't go away?

Chapter 5

It only took a few minutes to seem like I was walking around in one of those abandoned movie backlots. Old cinder block and brick buildings supported small hand painted signs and sat on quiet streets. Streets with no cars, no people, no fire hydrants, no vendor carts, and no telephone wires. The further my feet took me the odder the town became. Notwithstanding the lack of town decor but the lack of everything else pulled my attention. Trees. Shouldn't there be trees? Birds or dogs, cats, butterflies, something? Aside from the patches of grass passing for lawns the town seemed devoid of life, and color. Nearly everything was white washed or faded to a ghost town essence.

Every block of stores went on and on with other details missing, like houses, pharmacies, or cyclists being chased by annoying yapping dogs. Who exists in a place with none of that? I do, that's who. No pity parties please. I know my life's been abysmal and fairly vanilla when it comes to filling it with all those things Vanessa listed, but that doesn't mean my job doesn't hold meaning. I'm always on time and clean for work. I always finish every project and do every detail of my job spot on. Hell, I even run every errand they ask me to without question. So yeah, my home life might be a little shabby but my work life rocks.

Turning the corner onto Bell Avenue the buzzing in

my head came back full force, along with the annoying red dancing dots. Flashes of images from the office flooded forward along with something new - sound. Not just any sound but loud crunching as if dishes went suddenly crashing to the floor. Full-on Technicolor and screaming; lots of sudden intense screams. Maybe. I'm not sure. What I am sure of is waking up on a leather couch in a huge office with that guy who gave me the book sitting a few feet away.

"Feeling better?" a familiar voice asked, swinging the high back leather chair my direction. The three-piece suit he sported seemed more appropriate than trying to picture him in say jeans or a sweater. It gave him the appeal of an authoritative figure. Along with the slicked back almost perfect dark hair and crystal blue eyes, he'd pass for a corporate executive or spy thriller type. All that was missing was the cliche evil laugh.

"How'd you find me?" Vigilance tugged my senses and body out of the sleepy lethargy. That ever-present gnawing distrust reared its ugly head.

Clasping his hands before him, he leaned back with his elbows resting on the arms of the chair, "Henry went missing after I told him to bring you to work. And when you two didn't show, we got worried."

"I'm fine," I replied tersely, rubbing my eyes.

"But Henry's not. He's still missing." The seriousness of his tone and gaze set me off way before I knew it.

"He's a big boy. He'll find his way home." Was that really me being pissy with someone? I didn't like where my attitude was going and by the scrutiny on the guy's face, neither was he.

Rolling his eyes, he asked, "Wanna tell me why you decided to miss work this morning?" Steepling his fingers in front of his face, he waited patiently, something I didn't think was a fitting quirk of his. It didn't seem to match his bravado exterior.

"Look, I don't know you and I don't care. This is my dream and for some stupid reason, I'm still here. All of this is still here. I thought all this would be gone when I woke up this morning but..."

A knowing look finally settled between his creased brows, "I see." Reaching across the desk he pulled a file with my name on it and shuffled the papers, reading from a yellow one, waving one hand around. "You are convinced you're asleep and this, none of this, is real." It was my turn to roll my eyes. "Vanessa didn't explain your situation to you?"

"The nice blond lady in yellow with heels? Yes, she said I was in Limbo or something until my case is reviewed." Sitting up, I swung my feet to the floor, massaging my knee still aching from the night before. "But that doesn't explain any of this or why any of you are still here and I'm still not waking up."

"Because you're dead, as we've told you." It was cut

and dry, matter-of-fact. Casual. As if he were pointing out the obvious elephant standing alone in the middle of the empty circus tent to a child who still wasn't getting it. "I'm not supposed to give details, they're supposed to come to you on your own." Turning the yellow page he read from the back. "Do you remember your name yet?"

"Randy." There; that wasn't so hard. "Why couldn't I remember it yesterday?"

"Because that was yesterday," he said, as if reading my mind. Flopping back on the couch, my hand tapped the card in my pocket, making sure it was still there; more of a security blanket reassurance than anything. "Do you remember what you were doing last before emerging here?"

"I was at my desk downtown, working." Flashes popped like popcorn flooding my eyes. Straining to see them, they faded slowly. "What's going on? Why can I remember some things and others just fall away?"

"Everyone who enters the Bureau Wakening Room has amnesia. Some more severe than others, depending on how traumatic their incident. For instance, you met Flo yesterday, did you not?"

"Yeah. I remember her and everyone and everything from yesterday, but prior to that it's either a blur or fragments with screams."

Crossing his legs, he was at ease when he said, "Flo

55

didn't die of natural causes. She was stabbed several times during a robbery." Hearing him was akin to those vintage detective or spy shows from back in the day, when the bad guy would pull out a cigarette and get comfortable - right before they laid out the details of how you were going to fail your mission and die.

"She was robbed?" My eyes flew wide at the thought of the sassy redhead getting attacked by some behemoth and helplessly slaughtered.

"No, actually she was one of the robbers. Her partner, who was also her ex-husband, didn't want to share the haul, so he killed her." Now, I knew my head was shaking in disbelief but how was I supposed to know that sweet little old lady was a thief?

Muttering mostly to myself, I couldn't wrap my head around it, "She doesn't look like a robber."

"Because she has almost no memory of her former self. She knows she was really good at sewing, knitting, sculpting with clay, numbers and spatial recognition. But as for her life in crime, she draws a complete blank. She doesn't even get images or memories or feelings associated with it anymore. There's nothing to pull from so we closed her case with a reopenable option."

"How long has she been here?" Do I really want to know, or is my subconscious prying into things my waking self wanted to know about coworkers, but would never have the guts to ask? Should I even bother asking myself how screwed up I really am if I'm going to carry out therapy sessions in my sleep? Nah.

"She came through the Bureau doors maybe twenty years." My jaw dropped. I knew it because I felt it drop and there was no way I couldn't help but wonder if I was bug-eyed too. "She's done a lot over the years to learn her new trade. She takes a great deal of pride in her work. Her and the others."

I always wanted to be a journalist and that part of me reared its imprudent voice. "So there's more people stuck here than her?" I asked in a tone that implied I smelled a conspiracy cover up. I guess he's been here longer than I thought because he seemed to know that look too. And his response was more gentle and informative than I thought it would be.

The corners of his mouth pulled upward slightly, as if speaking to a child at first, but not condescending, "So to speak, yes. But I wouldn't use the term stuck. Makes it sound like there's no choice." Then he sighed the sigh of man with the weight of the afterworld on his shoulders, "No, our job is to help people get reoriented so they can piece together what happened to them, reconcile the last chapter of their life, and help them feel comfortable to move on."

"To here or there," I replied.

"That's right." The smile. The one he gives that creeps me out was back. The suit knew a lot more than what he was saying, but how much was he willing to give away? You could see it behind those intelligent eyes. "Then there are those, like Flo, who can't reconcile their past and stay on to learn a new life."

It sounded great, too great. The late night tv private eye inside me recoiled just a touch at the thought that I was treading on solid ground that'd been laid out professionally for a long time. And then there was the clerical side of me that had to match the numbers and have a perfect balance and saw it couldn't possibly be that simple.

With a click of a pen he snagged from the desk, he made quick notes inside the folder, bringing us both back to the moment, "Have you been blacking out lately?"

"No, not really." Okay, I admit I was being a bit cagey. But I wanted to err on the side of caution. My answers didn't really lie but at this point, I didn't know what to think or who to trust.

"Headaches? Pain? Nausea? Fever?" he asked, clicking the pen again.

"Just Headaches." No lies there, but that generic list could also have been for the flu.

"Flashes, memories, recollections or senses associated with your last moments?" Wow, he's thorough.

"Some, I suppose." I guess he suspected I wasn't being one hundred percent forthcoming since he closed the file and stared, as if boring a hole through me to the wall

58

on the other side a moment before making a decision.

"You don't trust me."

"Should I?" I have got to get that bug-eyed look under control. This time it was evident by the smirk he gave that this wasn't his first time dealing with a newbie.

"Rule No. 22 can get be hanged for now," he said with a deep breath. "I was a little pressed for time yesterday. I'm sorry. I'll start over for you." Coming to sit next to me he widened a soft grin, extending a hand, "Hello, my name's William Thorpe. It's a pleasure to meet you, Randy." Opening the file he let me read the information for myself.

The first three pages seemed to be copies of medical records from the hospital I was allegedly rushed to with admission notes stapled to the back of each one. It looked authentic, all the way down to the doctor's unidentifiable handwriting. But the notes were crystal clear and signed by a technician I remember I once dated, and her signature was always flawless.

There had been an accident, yet what kind was either ambiguous or missing from the front page. What stood out the most wasn't the gory details and pictures of how I arrived with my skull barely intact and dripping blood everywhere, or the description of my black and blue broken ribs bulging out to one side, or even the extensive journal of treatment and things they tried to save me, but the line at the bottom in a neat little box off to the left check marked T.O.D. signed by an ex-girlfriend, the technician, Felicia Stone - in flawless, perfect penmanship.

The niggling in the back of my mind finally settled and firmly rooted itself in justification for the images that'd been rising all morning; everything began to make sense. Waking to the feeling of loss yet being in a familiar environment somehow helped transition my brain and memories into a more stable pattern; something I could deal with and adapt to other than W.O.A.L. And I knew as I read, every word was true because I'd felt it; I'd lived it. The sounds of urgency had filled the space around me. I'd felt them stretching my aching sore jaw, shoving that tube down my throat so I could breath. I felt the sharp shooting pains in my chest and ribs as they cut into me and spread my chest apart, pushing and pulling with icicle fingers at my crackling bones. The sensations fleeting when I realized I could feel nothing, just like the nothingness between the surgical masks and gloves they wore and my own flesh and bones. I know because I felt and heard the high pitched squeal of the defibrillator as it sent shocks to my heart. I finally know, and remember, because I was aware of every single moment - until my last breath faded with their voices.

As I turned to Page 4 under the column marked Circumstance, in black and white was a bleak write up from Props Department:

Extensive injuries - cranial, internal, broken bones, massive blood loss. No major missing pieces or parts. See Props.

Missing: No watch, jewelry, glasses, or identifiable tattoos.

*Note: Nothing matching FBI, CIA, Interpol, or local authority databases.
Non-creative pomp; cliche - possible vehicular manslaughter.

Time/Date 08:37:33a 2017.04.01
Case: 08161986
Pending investigation

At the top right corner, yesterday's date and time had been stamped, but the second set of numbers next to it kept changing, blinking back at me. Keeping track of my time I suppose. Such a thick file for so little information. As my eyes scanned, rereading the notes and taking in the pictures, water trickled from them.

Uncomfortable much? Yep. Weirded out a little? Probably. Getting the creepy crawlies from realizing at this moment, this exact, precise moment - I'm officially dead? Definitely. And here I was, still waiting for the punchline, the hearty laugh to break the tension and defy my new reality; but the moment faded fast, and I knew it wasn't a joke. It turned into hearing that internal evil spy voice finally releasing his sinister laugh.

"Welcome to Limbo."

Chapter 6

"Funny, I don't feel dead," I mumbled, laying the folder gingerly on my lap, and drying my eyes with the back of my sleeve.

"Tell me about it." William sighed turning his back toward me, "See this?" Pointing to the back of his head he tilted forward a bit showing a thick white jagged scar running up the back of his neck into the hairline. "Props did the best they could but there's only so much that can be done when part of your spine is missing."

"Spine?" My brows shot upward, practically forgetting how moments ago I was blubbery and teary eyed over being pronounced dead and officially existing in this weird place.

"Yeah, someone made good on their threat to tear out my spine, literally. All I remember was stopping for gas at a station at night off of this little nowhere road and some guy jumped me. Made sure he shoved his knee in my back and my face to the ground and outright told me in my ear as plain as day, he'd come to collect." Involuntarily I reached for the back of my own head, feeling to see if everything was intact. "To this day I have no idea what that was about. It's one of the reasons I never left here. My file's been put on hold indefinitely," he admitted, forcing a smile through his gritting teeth. "And don't worry, Props did a great job restoring your features. At least your face is intact and you have most all your bones." My fingers involuntarily smoothed quickly over my face, not feeling any noticeable scars. I don't know what I was thinking. Maybe being afraid of looking like a hideous Franken monster with bolts protruding out the side of my neck holding my head to my shoulders; it was enough to strike a vanity vein in me. But it also made my thoughts land immediately to Vanessa. Maybe they did the best they could with her too.

"So, you're stuck - in Limbo?" It was a shadenfrauerer moment, and though it wasn't supposed to make me feel better, somehow knowing someone else's experience was way worse than mine did -- just a little.

"Well, yes and no. I could sign the paperwork to just leave, but justice wouldn't be served; and I'd really like to see the person who did this to me - get what they deserve." There was that look again. The predatory one. The one I always think 'shark' when I see it. To avoid becoming the guppy meant being friends with the shark, or at least find a way to be in the good graces of the predator, or make him forget I'm a guppy in his ocean. A minor tactical switch in subjects was in order.

"Why can't you remember? Why can't I?" I asked with short bursts.

"Good questions," he relaxed taking a deep breath, letting it out slowly as he sat back, the leather creaking beneath his weight. "Apparently, circumstances play a part. Some people are acutely aware of their existence the moment whatever happens to them and they carry it on afterward. Some are taken completely unaware and have no idea who they are or what's going on. Others like Henry didn't have much of a life to begin with. So, when they enter here..."

"They choose to stay because there's nothing to go back to?" Nodding at my remark, he shrugged. "Okay, then let me wrap my head around this...people die, they just show up at your office, and you present them with two choices -- sign off on their deaths so they can move on to whatever wherever, or don't and they get a chance to solve their own demise? And if either one doesn't happen, they get a job and stay here?"

"Relatively speaking, in an overly simplified manner, yes. Don't get me wrong, the system's not perfect. But it's the only one Limbo has and it works pretty well, if I do say so myself," he said wiping at a crease on his pant leg. "And for the record, people don't just show up at my office door waiting for me to hand out their death certificates. Those who come through the door at the Bureau's Awakening room go through a process to be revived. After a period of adjustment, they have the options of looking into their own cause of death or accepting what's on the paperwork. If they don't want to leave, they don't have to. They do have the option of staying. No one forces a person to stay against their will." Turning in his chair, William cocked his head to the side in quick thought, "As for your glasses and watch, Props couldn't put them back together so when they put only you back together the best they could. I have to confess, they tweaked you a bit. Your eyes did belong to someone else at one time but they're almost identical to your old ones. They're actually better, from what Morty says." I should be freaked out right now but the part of me that would normally be scrambling for the door sat firmly planted, listening, absorbing every detail.

Closing the file, the thought crossed my mind, "What happens if you remember or find out what happened to you? Is there some sort of trial or something you have to go through?"

"Nah. Just lots of paperwork and your signature. As long as you reconcile and accept the findings, it's a legit exit." William's grin tugged at the sides of his mouth tiredly. "We have investigators who are assigned case files. They find everything they can and try to close them quickly so people can get on with whatever lies ahead." Getting up from the couch he strolled over to lean on his desk. "Everything you can remember, any little detail, will help move your case to the front of the line. My suggestion? Read the manual, learn the rules, write down anything that might help you get through the day. Then, hopefully, soon enough, you can exit this place a happy man."

"Who's my case worker?"

"I'll have them get in touch with you in a couple of days. Meanwhile, skipping out on work may sound pleasant but at some point, it'd be nice for you to return and help out." I'm not so dead I can't recognize a gentle but subtle push when I hear one.

I've gotta say, there's something seriously wrong with me. While part of my brain wants to run off and ditch anything that resembles work, there's a stronger part of my mind that sees this pleading look he's giving me, "I don't even know what I'm doing. The paperwork looks familiar but..." and I suddenly want to help.

"Because it is. It's more like your old job than you realize. Budgets need organization here too and you're the first person in almost five years to come through who can do it in his sleep - literally." Hope is the killer of laziness. The hope in his eyes was selling it, and worse, he knew it.

"Then I *am* in hell." This time William burst, chuckling. As I got up, I tucked the folder under my arm and headed toward the door. "You know, I haven't had a vacation in years. What does a guy have to do to get one? Be here like six months for a week off or what?"

"Nothing so dramatic." Pulling another file William handed me a simple form. "Fill this out and state how long you want off and when you want to take it, then bring it back to me."

"What if I don't want to work? What if I just want to laze around and maybe find out what happened to me?" There I go, trying to weasel my way out.

"Then you still have to fill out the form." Oh, the look of sympathy I automatically gave him. I get it. He's the guy who ultimately has to deal with all the paperwork. I suppose it's easier to have a trail and keep track of it, but still. Paper for everything? I only died a couple of days ago. Things haven't changed that much.

"Why don't you have computer's to do this?" I genuinely wanted to know. Someplace this convoluted with rules that read like a government manual seemed like it really needed computers.

"Budget and IT. We don't have anyone dead who could install or fix one."

"That stinks," I replied honestly.

"Tell me about it," he sympathized with a quick roll of his eyes, waving me out the door. "Oh and the file needs to stay here. If you want, I can get you a copy of everything inside."

"Can you have it sent to my apartment?'

"Sure," he said picking up his pen. "When we find Henry, he can drop it by."

"One more thing..."

"You're full of questions - shoot, proverbially," the pen in his hand clicked habitually. I couldn't tell if he was annoyed I was still there or just being helpful.

"Why is it the town seems abandoned? I saw tons of stores and buildings just sitting empty. No lawns, birds, anything. Or let me guess, budget?" This time his reaction was like an inside joke shared between us.

"Mainly because of the budget. We only have so much room to work with and when someone leaves, we have to reuse what we have and make accommodations when and where we can. That includes workplaces and homes; you have no idea how much work has to be done in a short amount of time to get everything prepped for just one person let alone if we get a slew of them coming in all at once. As for animals, we don't get many through here; we're not exactly sure why. The theory is that they've already reconciled their departures so they have no qualms moving on. Occasionally a pet is so completely devoted, they end up following their masters here. The problem is, the animal can't sign off its death acceptance, so when the owner signs, the animal has to leave with them. Is that all?"

"For now." Sitting in his leather high back chair he smirked kindly. Laying the folder on the corner of his desk, I reached for the door.

"Are you sure you weren't a lawyer?" he teased. But my subtle grin and roll of the eyes said plenty as the door shut behind me.

If it'd been any other day, I'd say screw it - gonna grab a sandwich and go to the park. Except, there might not be a park to go to and I'm starting to wonder where the food comes from? Best not go there. If I wonder too hard, it'll make me look for answers and I'm not sure I'm ready for that yet. Maybe that's why I'm dead. I mean, maybe I walked out in front of a bus because I wasn't paying attention or something. Or did I drive off the road asleep at the wheel? Any number of things could have happened, and any number of them could have simply been my fault.

Ever get that nagging sensation you forgot something important back home? Like you left the stove top on or maybe you didn't turn off the lights behind you as you grabbed the keys and ran out? That's what it feels like. Only I'm pretty sure I wasn't driving or outdoors. So why do I feel like I got run over by a bus? Better yet, why do I hear screams when I close my eyes? Is it me screaming or someone else? There's that nagging sensation again - like I left the lights on back home.

Well, I guess I could go search for Henry; he couldn't have gotten far. Maybe that'll earn me some brownie points with Vanessa and William. I need to find him a nickname. William's just so - formal. But I can't just go around calling him big Willie or Bill or Billy, or even Mac. I don't think I can even call him Mr. Thorpe; he just doesn't seem like a Thorpe to me. He strikes me more of a Casini or Kirkman. More posh than something normal. I'll think of something.

Chapter 7

And low, thereupon the steps after a couple of hours of searching sat a lost and bewildered man. "Dude, where you been? William's been looking all over for you."

Startled, Henry's face lit up like a Christmas tree as I stepped from the curb crossing the street, looking both ways, just in case. "I've been around." he shrugged, standing quickly, tucking an envelope beneath his arm. "Saw a few things. Boy, am I glad I still have my card," he said, practically bouncing on his toes. "I have no idea what I'd do if I lost that."

"Can't you just get a new one if you do?"

"Rule No.33. Lose it - break it - forget it, there are no replacements. Pretty much, you're screwed."

"I...see." I guess the tone of my voice carried both a question and answer from the look he gave me.

"It's no big deal, I mean, I can't remember anyone ever losing one," he said. Irony: the time it took for the statement to register and the exact moment I tried not laughing. "Well, you know what I mean."

Pocketing my hands I turned in one spot, looking the street over. Except for the fact that the building sticks out like a black and white photo has been touched up with a splotch of color; it actually looks to be a normal red brick building with plants in some windows and clothes hanging out others. Similar to the two people I'm pretty sure are either following or watching me a block away. It's hard to tell but when there's color in a gradient black and white place, you notice.

"Wanna come up for lunch?" I offered.

"Really?!" Enthusiasm and honesty. Couldn't ask for more.

"Sure. Come on up." I'm not certain why I asked a complete stranger to come to my apartment. Safety in numbers maybe? I don't even know if I have groceries. Hell, I don't even know if I have a refrigerator. But as the key card slid through the lock and the door opened, I heard a click that wasn't the lock and had seconds to move, which was not enough.

Being bowled over and landing on my back sent the sudden huff of wind right out of my lungs. Somewhere downstairs was the echo of voices yelling, reverberating off the walls.

"Stop! Halt!" Slamming doors and footsteps running was all I heard. Thankfully, there weren't any gunshots; that would've freaked me out worse than I already am.

"Holy crap! You okay?" Henry knelt beside me, helping me up as I dusted off my pants.

"Yeah, I think so." Pocketing my card we looked over

the balcony to the lower level. Light streaming in from outside lessened as the main door squeaked closed in their wake. "Who the hell was that? What was he doing in my apartment?"

"Dunno," Henry said, peering over the banister. "But at least whoever was following you took off after the guy. There's that," he shrugged indifferently.

"So I've got some creepy spooks tailing me, people breaking into an apartment that has next to nothing in it, and I've only been here one day?" I snarled pursing my lips, my backside feeling the wannabe bruise coming up.

"Spooks?" Henry asked innocently, his brow rising at the word.

"Yeah, you know. People meant to be invisible like ghosts to walk among us. It's what I think the CIA used to call operatives or something." The mildly lost sentiment in his shifting eyes was the first clue to change the subject. "I guess that word could have been a little insensitive with the whole dead, ghost, spook thing," I said wearily, swearing under my breath while fidgeting with the door handle. "Sorry."

"You make enemies as fast as you make friends?" he asked, casting a questioning glance my way.

"Dunno. I've never really had friends." Maybe I shouldn't have admitted that, but then again, "or enemies, for that matter."

"What about frenemies? Got any of those?" he quirked. The tugging at the corners of my mouth turned up at his words. Squirming in my own skin was not the kind of reaction I wanted to present so going with pleasant seemed right. "Do we need to write a report or fill out a form or something?"

"I have no idea. Honestly, I've only been here one day so I couldn't even tell ya if I have food."

Henry has that type of face that makes you think, 'Wow, what a nice guy and safe to be around'. Kinda the boy next door who never gets the girl but is always the best friend when you need one. That's the vibe I get from him, which makes me wonder if he had a wife or girlfriend before he died.

"Hey, look at that! A refrigerator," he jived poking me in the arm and laying down the envelope. "Open it. Let's see whatcha got." Yeah, it was also like being around an eleven-year-old who still believed Christmas and the wonders of the world.

"Wouldn't ya know. It's empty," I said. Priceless. The look on his face slid to a sad puppy look; I couldn't keep jesting. "Just kidding. Looks like sandwich meats and bread, some mayo."

"That's fine," he said eagerly pulling up a bar stool to the kitchen counter, restlessly thrumming his fingers. "So, you've only been here a day." Small talk was never one of my better qualities and apparently, it wasn't one of his.

74

"Yeah."

"Whaddaya think of the place? Limbo, I mean." With a lack of eye contact and cloddish sentences, I'd take a wild guess he hadn't had many people to talk to in his life, or death. Then again, his story may be as unusual as Flo's, assuming he remembers any of it.

"It's okay, so far." Non-committal shrugging. That thing people do when they don't want to tell the truth or when they don't know how much to say. And it was that thing I was doing to avoid putting myself in an uncomfortable conversation. "Henry, if you have something you want to say or ask, just do it. I won't be offended as long as you stay away from relationships, those are taboo."

"Uh-kay," tapping the countertop harder Henry stared at one spot, practically burning a hole through the wood in thought. "Do you remember anything before yesterday?"

"Not yet but I get these images and sounds I can't make out." I shrugged again, slopping on the mayo and cheese. "I'm trying hard to remember but..."

"You busy later?" he interrupted.

"Asking me out already?" I replied handing over the sandwich. Didn't even phase him, and that was one of my best attempts at a joke.

"Just wanna show you where I went earlier." It wasn't what he said, it was the way he said it and the ominous carrot-dangling promise in those glassy eyes.

"Okay. I'm down with that. How about after lunch?" I'm not very good at reading people but if I were any judge of character, I'd say something was gnawing at him. His eyes darting around the kitchen and living room while tearing off large chunks of the sandwich, looking over his shoulder - literally. "Slow down Henry. Chew your food. Maybe taste it the first time around." Shifting his weight uneasily on the stool, he swallowed then went after the glass of water being handed off to him. "Seriously, I don't want to have to explain to someone how you choked to death in my apartment." That got a grin.

"Yeah," he said finally working the food between his teeth. "There's way too much paper involved."

Uncomfortable silence. That long pause where the conversation takes a turn into a dead end or cul-de-sac. Just when I thought I was the ultimate introvert, I come up against someone who is almost a mirror of myself, or worse. Someone else with a broken filter for what comes naturally to others when it comes to societal norms, like chit chat.

"Not to change the subject but did you recognize any of those people?" I finally asked, cleaning the counter. Why I'm taking better care of this apartment when I didn't even make my bed in the other life is beyond me. Existential crisis - does it exist for us in Limbo? I mean, if this is an afterlife, what's the other called? Pre-afterlife? Just life? Isn't that a little narrow-minded? Don't people here live mostly like we did in the other life? Okay, I need to get a grip. I'm starting to have what...a life crisis, death crisis? Overthinking. Just overdoing it a bit. Relax. Deep breath. Exhale. I hadn't realized I'd been staring down at the counter breathing deep and long until Henry tapped my shoulder.

"Did you hear me?" he repeated.

"Sorry, what?" Shaking the cobwebs from the old brain attic, I threw back most of my glass of water in a few of gulps.

"I said, there were two people that kept checking the neighborhood today; it might of been the ones who ran from your place just now. They'd walk by, take notes and leave. I think I saw them again just before you arrived."

"But you don't know either of them?" My mind reeled with more questions but they slipped away the moment he answered - nope. "Would it be alright if we postponed this little trip until after dinner? I'd like to get caught up on a few things around here first, like reading some of those rules everyone seems to know but me."

"Yeah, no problem. I'll meet you out front later. By the way, the envelope is from Will. Says you requested it. See ya!" After the door clicked shut and the quiet of the room started to feel like it was physically pressing in on my skin, I turned to find a radio, television, anything for some white noise. But those too were missing from here.

"What? They got something against prime time and music? Sheesh!" At least the couch was semi-comfortable, even if the springs were poking me almost identical to my old one. Which, is needless to say, I do not miss.

The book started reading just like a government manual from line one page one, except without the legal mumbo jumbo:

Rule No.1: The Dead are to remain dead.

Pardon me if duh is all I can say to that.

Rule No.2: The Deaf can hear, don't talk too much to them; the Blind can see, don't wave them down;
the Mute can talk so don't let them talk too much or they'll literally talk your head off.

Who writes this crap? Reminds me a little of Morty and Art though.

Rule No.3: Refill the coffee maker. If you drink it, refill it.
Isn't that just a peach. Someone really thinks these things through. Then again, I've been on the receiving end of someone's tirade when the coffee maker was empty and they saw me drink the last cup. Okay, maybe there's a little validity, but to actually write it in a manual?

The more I read, the more I questioned the authenticity and sanity of the author. Page after page read like a technical manual or a step by step guide to building a child's playhouse. Simple on some levels and complex as hell on others and always out of order.

Rule No. 88 Copiers, printers, fax machines, phones, and other essential or non-essential office or non-office equipment shall be maintained and stored in proper cooling facilities and recommended a PAT (Potential Asset Tag). Each PAT is to be inventoried and reconciled on page 5 in goldenseal triplicate then turned into Home at the beginning of each quarter.

Ugh! If I weren't already dead the zombie reading would be killing me. More classical bureaucratic bs, shoveling paper in the afterlife, just like the other life. I guess it's true, you really can't hide or run away from your destiny. It finds you in every dark corner and patch of sketchy sunlight, no matter if you're here or there. Damn, now they've got me saying it.

Putting the book down on the floor I rubbed tired, gritting eyes. There was just so much even I could take. Time to see if what was spooking Henry was going to sidetrack my inevitable lovely mental breakdown.

Chapter 8

At least the day wasn't a total bust. I had found Henry safe and sound; nothing was broken when the perps bowled me over in their rush to leave, and nothing's missing that can be seen - then again, I'm not sure I'd know since I haven't inspected the place well yet. And as a bonus, I may have made a new friend in Henry. But I still don't know who was following me or yelling just now. all in all someone might say good luck had my back, but it could also be argued that bad luck is what got me killed.

My cynicism reared its ugly head to put its two cents worth in. Huh, luck. Laughable. Good or bad, it hasn't helped me; or any of these people, for that matter. How would luck be measured for us, them, me? We're all dead. That can't be too lucky. Looking at Flo's life, it could be shrugged into a neat package of good luck that her death got her out of a life of crime. But for me? I'm almost certain I wasn't a gangster, thief, or politician. How do I know? Because, it's something inside me, I can feel. Sensing who you are and what you aren't can be just as important as asking the right questions to the right people in the right way. For instance, how'd William know how long she's been here? Answer: the same as on my file; a little time/date stamp on the information sheet. Watching the numbers move on the paper next to the area labeled for when I arrived here was disturbing but informative.

There's something else that's been bothering me other than a lack of glasses - I didn't realize until a moment ago, my watch is missing too. And not having seen any way of telling time other than sun up, sun down, and night time gets a little frustrating. It's like being in a casino with almost no windows and no sense of time, other than when you have to go to the bathroom or eat.

In the short span of observing this place, the questions have started accumulating rather than being answered; and I hate loose ends; the way things tend to dangle unfinished. No one lets a barber or hair stylist get away with sorta giving a cut or shave. Nah. People bitch and complain to the high heavens if the product isn't complete. No one walks around with seventy percent of a cut, six out of ten fingernails painted, one of two shoes shined, laundered shirts pressed but still showing the stains. People would raise holy hell if they went to a ball game and only got seven innings out of nine, or the person runs down the basketball court leaving everyone else in the dust, only to get lined up with the hoop and stand there not taking the shot. My point is, this place feels unfinished.

When Henry left, he made sure to leave me with a few of those brain itchers. "Time's a funny thing," he said, "we're so conscious of it when we're traipsing around living, breathing. Can't tell ya how long I've been here and I know deep down inside, I had a time sensitive job - just don't remember what it was." As he turned the handle to my door, he stared down at the floor,

"Ever wonder where the food comes from? I may not remember much, but I remember what a restaurant looks like."

And there it was, the dangling carrot of details unanswered. Cryptic and subtle. The anal retentive part of me screamed, 'Why on earth would you do this to me? Don't I have enough to worry about, like finding out why I'm dead?' Yeah, he knew I'd show up at sundown if for nothing more than to settle the ledger in my head from going all red. Everything must be in black, balanced, and mean something. He knew what he was doing, sly dog.

Ever see those late, late, late night shows that come on after one in the morning when everything else has gone off the air? This was one of those cheesy B-rated moments spawned from the memory of a classic scene where the warehouse is enshrouded with thick rolling fog, and our would-be misfit heroes literally quake in their shoes at the sound of all too loud crickets and overly noisy bushes. You know, the one where two people who shouldn't be somewhere snap open a padlock when the security guards are off somewhere unknown. And inside they discover weird experiments gone wrong just before one of those experiments, usually a werewolf, jumps from an incredibly high stack of crates to land on the unsuspecting expendable characters, tearing them to shreds along with the evidence of its existence. And even though there are no crickets and I'm fairly certain no werewolves, and we aren't a couple of would-be heroes; we were still creeping around trespassing in the middle of the night asking for trouble. Yep, I watched a lot of tv and that's exactly where my imagination went, and ratcheted up the anxiety pumping through every vein in my body, as we approached the district two streets behind my apartments.

Another few blocks up and there he was bouncing on his toes like a kid on sugar overload, waiting for me.

"Seriously? The card doesn't work on this thing?" My voice quivered, shoving my cooling hands into my pants pockets for warmth as he put his keycard away. The last image I caught on it was a stick figure with my name coming to stand in proximity to him, then vanished as we spoke. Pulling out an odd piece of material he unrolled it in one hand. With the other, he picked out a thin metal rod no longer than a pen with a flat hook on the end.

"Nah, this gate and facility predate that technology, I think." Henry huffed, shoving the lock aside with a quick few flips of his wrist and the soft sound of a latch releasing.

"You can pick locks? Is that illegal here?" My fine sense of justice didn't know the rules or boundaries of Limbo and didn't really want to find out. But pleading the Fifth didn't seem like an option either after I practically aided and abetted him.

"Yep," Henry quirked stowing the tools away, "and nope. It's just something I can do. That a problem?" Great. Maybe he's another Flo and doesn't know it.

"Nope." What is it with me? He's grinning proudly, standing there holding open the gate that I'm walking through like we didn't just commit breaking and entering. Did I do this sort of thing before I died? Would I have actually have gone along with something like this without batting an eyelash? "Let's see what you've got." Who am I?

Chapter 9

About half the size of the warehouse on Cragston and Shirley, and just as dark, stood a half empty storage room with a humming generator the size of a car sitting against the back wall. The nearly overwhelming smell of coffee permeated the building as we stepped inside. To the left jutted breaker boxes and cages around them to keep them safe; from whom or what I can't imagine since there's next to nobody in this part of town.

Treading lightly, the echoes of our footsteps became dampened by the dust-laden floor. In all the places I've been in my life, I've never seen facilities so poorly taken care of. Normally there'd be a janitor or someone to sweep the place, keep it tidy and free of things that can cause slippage; apparently, Limbo has a lack of talent for some of the simpler things, like a broom and someone to use it.

Not having night vision goggles or super powers that might help me see in the dark was a little more than annoying. But then again, I'm not a hero with unlimited money at my disposal or a vigilante with powerful friends who have powerful gadgets. But, there's no need to be a superhero with extraordinary powers when someone, namely me, can recognize another set of footprints blazing a trail off to our right. Ahead stood aisles of boxes and pallets of what looked like the outlines of computers neatly piled and office equipment stacked on them.

"I thought William said they couldn't afford any of

this stuff. It's practically new; well, newish, at least within the last couple of years or so." Shaking a small cardboard box, the contents rattled, spilling everything from paper clips and pens to paper and receipt books on top of the stack of boxes. "Why lie if you can use this stuff?" The next two small boxes were packed with loose coffee beans, giving off a strong aroma.

"That's not what I wanted to show you." Henry pointed to the door furthest to the right where the line of footprints stopped and a faint glow shown beneath. As the handle to the door turned, squeaking its alarm, we dodged behind the nearest pallet of equipment. The smell of Chinese food and burgers wafted down the aisle making my bottomless pit of a stomach gurgle and ache for another meal. The door to the room opened far enough to let the little Asian lady from my apartment step through, tapping it shut with her shoulder behind her. The large order of food stacked in her dainty hands tipped this way and that before she got both hands around it, securing it with each step and laying it on the table. Wiping her hands on her jeans she turned to the door and went back through. This time, it stayed open longer, slowly closing with the long squeak of rusting hinges unseen. On the other side, the sounds of people speaking a mixture of Spanish, English, and maybe Chinese could barely be overheard. Her voice had become distinct among them, laughing at something one of them had said. In seconds an elderly man whose face looked like a deeply tanned Shar Pei puppy escorted our Evey to the portal where she came back through with more carry out containers. As she turned to close the door, the elderly man spoke something that sounded harsh and made her turn back to him with a grimace and a hard look that should have had him shaking where he stood. I know I was. Just then his eyes flicked toward the kitchen around them and back to her, waiting. Neither of us wanted to be in the middle of something awkward but there we were. As I shuffled my feet uncomfortably, crouching further, Evelyn reached out with a hand as fast as a snake and smacked the guy on the arm, saying something in his language back to him before barking out a laugh. The two hugged and parted ways as what I'm going to call friends because honestly, I think those two have known each other a long time. Or at least I hope so.

"Funny man. I show him who smell like great-grandmother," she mumbled shuffling to the table. "Use soap next time I bathe. HA! Funny man." Evelyn smiled as she laid down the rest of the containers and ensured the portal closed.

I kinda felt bad as I crouched there watching her struggle to get the other door to the storage facility open by herself. Henry didn't say it out loud but his body language said it for him. He didn't want to help her or be behind that pallet. Visible beads of sweat began to drench his forehead as we watched and waited. Personally, I wanted to jump out and maybe offer to get the door or assist in her deliveries, but if either of us stepped forward, we'd be caught without a solid plan; so chivalry was off the table tonight. Shaking my head, I caught him gesturing toward her. Making the 'head sliced off' signal with my hands, he sagged back against the computers, shifting them a few inches. For a brief moment, the little Asian lady paused, cocking her head to the side and listened. I felt my heartbeat increase as she shuffled toward us slowly. Holding perfectly still, Henry closed his eyes, not daring to breathe too hard. After a moment, she shrugged and made her way back through the door leaving us to exhale deep and strong. Sagging back, Henry nodded toward the pallet behind me. Nestled among the machines seemed to be smaller coffee cans left partially open on more stacks of computers. Throwing a surprised look my way we both shrugged and quietly decided it was best not to touch anything else. Besides, as soon as the door clicked into place, we scrambled to the one she'd come out of and used my key card to reopen.

The greasy handle slipped through my fingers with ease. Wiping them on my shirt, we snuck into the tiny offset room. Along one wall stood stacks of food on a long plastic table that may have once been white; it was impossible to tell from all the stains and smears across the warped surface. And apparently they don't have repairmen or a maintenance crew here since two of the legs of the table were being held up by old hard drives and an overturned bowl.

Before us stood an arrangement of blinking lights on a console with switches, buttons and the works; as if it was something from an old Sci-Fi movie with a low budget for props. But what really stood out was another door standing all by itself to our right. Not as part of a wall or attached to anything, just — standing there, emanating a soft electric blue glow around its creases and cracks.

"Is this what you wanted to show me?" the tremor in my voice grew dry as I coughed on the last words.

"Actually," Henry thumbed back toward the first door, "I was just going to show you the tire tracks and an old army truck around back. I haven't been in here before, but it's kinda cool." That little kid grin of his was going to get us in serious trouble.

"Yeah Henry, cool. But what is it?" I asked, staring wide eyed. "What kind of place is this?"

"It no place for you, dat what!" The clipped voice of the little Asian lady meant she was back, and standing right behind us. She needs to wear a cowbell or something; let people know she's around before we jump completely out of our skins. "How you get in here?" Showing her my card she nodded curtly. "Dey finally send me help. 'Bout time." Exchanging glances, I spoke up, cutting whatever Henry was about to say off.

"Yes. You're overwhelmed with deliveries so we're here to help. Right Henry?" I said in my most convincing boy scout tone.

Nodding wordlessly he swallowed hard, "What he said."

"Don't be 'fraid to learn sumting new. Took me few weeks but here I am. Now here you are." What a nice way to sucker a couple of suckers into helping her. Not that I wouldn't have but it was the best I could come up with under the circumstances and by the 'what the hell are you doing' look Henry's giving me, I'm sure I'll hear about it. "You two grab bags, bring wit me. I gotta load dem fast. Fast, fast! Dey hot!"

In moments, we walked to a part of the warehouse neither one of us had seen. Outside sat a golf cart we helped load with precision and speed as she beckoned us to move quicker. She must've had it stashed somewhere along the corner of the building earlier or in a shed or something because it didn't come from where we came in.

"Thank you. You two my lil helpers." Such a lovely smile. Such a lovely quaint accent. Such a lovely wave of her hands as she loaded the last of her deliveries and escorted us out what was missed the first time as an official exit, around the front of the building. In our haste to scope out the place, we hadn't investigated far enough around to find the front gate which stood wide open at some unattended guard shack. "You come back? You help Evey?"

"Yeah, no problem. Same time?" I asked enthusiastically as she nodded, waved absently and went happily on her way. "You heard the lady, same time tomorrow night," I said tapping him with the back of my hand on his chest.

"I can't," Henry stammered walking around in circles, wringing his hands. "I won't. I can't. It's wrong." I didn't need special comic book senses to figure out he was more than a little anxious and ready to put those hands to use around my neck. For some reason, I was trusting him not to act on that impulse. But just in case, the thought had crossed his mind, I made sure I backed up a couple of feet - just to stay out of arm's reach.

"What? You got plans or a date or something?" I know I was being cynical and maybe a little pushy but my brain decided it was better to attack than defend, "You brought me here, remember? We need to find out what's going on with that door and we won't find out unless we come back tomorrow night. She'll suspect something's wrong if we both don't show up. Right?"

Sweaty palms, erratic eye movement, pacing. Henry was going to give himself a heart attack and me anxiety if he didn't slow down. "Mad at me?" I asked, putting my hands up in a defensive gesture. There was something in the way he watched my body language that made him sulk then drop his shoulders, apparently changing his mind. A look of maybe concern or confusion, or both? Henry's a little hard to read sometimes. Not that I've ever been great at that sort of thing but, if there's anything I've learned is that he projects his thoughts loud and clear. You never really have to second guess with him.

"Yeah, I am. But, you're right," he sighed scrubbing his face in his hands as we watched the little golf cart disappear down the street into the night. Not that anyone could tell where she went since the street lights don't seem to work either. Total darkness and no crickets, owls, or raccoon to break the silence. Man, this world sucks.

"So we have one question answered, the food doesn't come from UFOs, it really is delivered. The problem is, who pays for it?" Rubbing my chin the idea came to me, "If William's department is paying, where'd they get the money?"

Squirming his shoulders, Henry made this gurgling sound lightly in the back of his throat, "I'm not exactly comfortable talking about money and UFOs in the same sentence." The blush was genuine and so was his kicking a foot toward innocent pebbles on the ground. It wasn't just some boyish innocent, charming thing he had going for him. No, he was the real deal. And I was still learning his quirks. Like now, for instance. I could be nosy and ask him about his UFO qualifications just to see if he's one of those who believes in little green men from Mars, but it's more of a feeling I get from listening to him. As if he'd been part of something in the government that might have been a coverup, or he knew things but just couldn't remember them clearly. Maybe that's why he either can't or won't talk about it. But does that make me a jerk for wanting to know?

"And just how many UFO's do you think this place deals with? Or aliens, for that matter?" I snapped, wishing instantly I hadn't. "Look man, I'm sorry. I was just trying to let you see there's nothing here that's dangerous. No little green men with lasers, no unidentifiable disks floating in the air and zipping off at high speed, and no conspiracy theories about them." I held up my hand in a scout's honor salute and he acknowledged it forgivingly-

barely.

"Fine, no aliens and no government conspiracies. But where do you suppose that thing goes?" he asked while giving a curt nod over my shoulder.

"What? The door?" Passive and nonchalant; that's what Henry needed, so that's what I gave him, something to diffuse the tension he was radiating and help calm his jangled nerves. "Eh, it's a door. You go through, get food, come back. Simple. And something about Rule 4."

"But Rule No. 16." Yeah, I rolled my eyes at him and deserved the rebuttal, "Clearly you haven't read the book yet. Have you even cracked it open?" It's amazing how fast he can change his attitude and moods, paranoid and insecure to cranky and a disappointed mom tone in under six seconds.

"Yeah, yeah. I've been reading it. Sorta. The damn thing reads like a technical manual," I shot back. "And for your information, Rule 4 applies here, close the door. I get it."

"What am I going to do with you?" Henry asked, shaking his head in mild disgust. "Rule 16 clearly states you shouldn't interact with the living. It's prohibited. It's also why Rule 4 is in place. It's not just to keep us from staying there. It's also so they don't come here. The doors go both ways."

"But why not? She did. She clearly broke that rule.

And talked to people, and made them laugh. I'm sure that's against the rules somewhere." I hate conflict. I don't like the way I feel when someone else can make a rule and break the same rule they expect me to follow. And then there's the part that slipped, "Wait, what? You said doors, plural. There's other doors?"

"Duh, of course. What'd you think? There's only one door in and out to this place? There's portals in at least six other places in this part of town that I know of, or at least that I remember." Suddenly the tops of his shoes became very interesting to him as his eyes fixated on their laces. "Oh come on man, everybody knows why." Pursing his lips tight, the weight shifted on his feet. For once, I was the kid being spoken to in the parental tone.

"And?" I pushed, feigning indifference.

"It's Evey. She's the only one I know of that comes and goes without restrictions. And no, I don't know or don't remember why the reset of us can't; you just don't. I read it somewhere in the manual. But take my word for it. Maybe if you try to go back into the living world you'd cause problems for the people who had to let you go? So people don't have to go through the awful pain of losing you again and again. Once is enough. Personally, I wouldn't do that to anyone I knew or loved." I had to admit, that made sense. But what if you had no one? Could you go back? Could you continue your life or pick up another one? "Stop that right now," he warned shaking a stern finger toward me.

"Stop what?" Play dumb and innocent, you know you can when you need to.

"That! That thinking thing you do. I can see the cogs turning in your eyes and it's not good. It's never good!" he grumbled.

"Henry, what if you could go back?" I pleaded, "What if you're not meant to spend eternity in Limbo? What would you do if you could walk through that door and pick up where you left off, or start something new? Wouldn't it be worth it?" The crazed look of barely coming across as sane registered somewhere in my thoughts. Much the same realization as I just saw on Henry's face. "Look, all we have to do is go along with this for a while and help the lady out. Maybe learn a little about that door and how this all works. All I'm asking is for you to meet me here again tomorrow night. We don't have to do anything more than that. It's not like we have plans after dark anyway."

Sagging his shoulders in melodramatic defeat, he kicked at the innocent pebbles harder, scattering them into the echoey shadows. "Fine! But I'm telling you this doesn't feel right. It's like I'm lying or something."

"How's it lying?" my voice rose in indignant levels. "We're here to help her get the deliveries together and loaded. You saw her struggling with the boxes. We're her assistants. Besides, if we happen to be left unchaperoned to investigate this place, how's that anyone's fault but theirs?"

The cogs behind his eyes like the ones in cartoons, if they could be seen, would have had steam and smoke billowing from their rusty mechanisms. "It just is," he mumbled. "I don't have to like it."

"Good man! Now, meet me in front of my apartments tomorrow night and we can walk here together," I said more cheerfully than I should have.

"Why can't I just meet you here?" the drop in Henry's voice had become more sullen.

"Believe it or not, this place creeps me out after dark. Not just the warehouse but the whole town. Like there's something evil lurking in the shadows waiting to swallow you whole." Staring into the night, Henry visibly swallowed against whatever my imagination was cooking up to spook us both. "Look, I'm sure there's nothing here that'll hurt us, I promise. It's just not what I'm used to and my imagination tends to make worse case scenarios in the form of late night B rated television reruns. We're already dead. What could possibly happen after you're dead?"

"Famous last words," he muttered, lacing his hands briefly behind his head, laying it back to view a silky black expanse blanketed with flickering and pulsating brilliant flashes from the stars above. "I'll be here." Pushing his hands into his pockets, Henry left me standing at the gates, his silhouette blending into the night with little to no sounds left behind.

Chapter 10

"Whoever left the coffee on overnight is in serious trouble!" Vanessa would have looked more pissed off if her facial muscles could actually move more, but everyone got the message. Her shrill tone cut through my skull making even me shrink back, and I'm not the one who left it on. "Rule No. 3 people! If you drink it, replace it. Not difficult!" Behind my hands, I hid the giggle at her ranting fury. She wasn't wrong, but she also wasn't right. It was a coffee drinker's worst nightmare, being out of the liquid sustenance and having what was left burned to the bottom of the carafe. She's lucky it didn't burst from the heat.

Viewing the faces of what I started calling interns hustling to get their work done, began becoming more familiar. The same group came by almost every hour doing routine office work, then they'd all leave and go to wherever it is their work takes them. Part of me wonders where that is but there's no time to follow around a bunch of pups running errands.

Pulling open a set of files, my eyes scanned, paying closer attention to the receipts and expenditures. Not to brag, but in my living job, I was one helluva clerk - I think. The memories are actually tangible today. The more I slow down and actually do the job, the more aware I am. That sounds stupid but, facts are facts; they don't change because you want them to.

Every file has its own unique content, like a

fingerprint, it can't be duplicated or changed, but it can be manipulated. Stowing a recent stash of files aside, I waited until the fourth round of interns finished their tasks and exited with Vanessa hot on their heels before I made my way down the hall. Opening the last door on the left, I poked my head in, hoping he was available. "Hey there, got a sec?"

Pulling tired eyes up from his work, William greeted me with that salesman smile, "Randy! Come on in. What can I help you with?"

"I have some questions about these files," I said, setting them on his desk where he could read. "The odd thing I can't wrap my head around is this figure at the bottom. It stays the same no matter what's on the receipts or invoices. It should reflect what's been bought and how the money comes in." On that note, I paused chewing at my bottom lip, "William, where is the money?" Standing he made his way to the door, shutting it quietly with a soft click.

"You're way too good at your job. Know that?" he said walking over to prop himself on one corner of the desk. "It comes in on a timetable and is kept in the bank. What we're concerned with is the balance at the bottom. It needs to reflect the same at the bottom of the sheet as the receipts subtracted show at the top."

"But they don't." There I go again, opening my mouth faster than my brain can work. "I mean, I tallied this months and the figures are off by a lot."

"How much are we talking?" William's voice dropped nearly a full level.

"This month? Almost ten thousand. The last six months I've gone through, I've seen a trend of eight to thirteen thousand. I'd have to re-balance previous months to tell you if there's more or just a glitch but it looks like money's being skimmed or just misplaced. My personal opinion? I'd say it's being funneled slowly and hidden somehow. Numbers don't lie." Now, this seemed familiar. It sounded a lot like a conversation I'd previously had with someone who sounded a lot like William. It even feels like I've lived this moment before. But that reeling sense of deja-vu would have to wait for me to wake up. The floor spun as my ears rang in a high pitch, sending the ceiling into weird shapes and colors. The image of William's wall burst into splinters as glass exploded around me, sending me into darkness.

Gentle tapping against my cheek, repeatedly, insistently became annoying. Nope, I didn't want to wake up, but I also didn't want to keep getting nearly slapped either. The cool weight against my eyes kept them from opening until the cloth had been lifted.

"Randy, open your eyes." William's voice came from next to me urgently, "I need you to focus on my voice. You can do it." There ya smug bastard, they're open.

Pulling a cold wet cloth from my face, he set it aside. A light ringing in my ears faded while my voice cracked as

I tried to sit up, "What the hell?"

"Not so fast. Lay there and try to remember what you saw," he said, studying me with those intense shark like features. Okay, maybe he doesn't look like a shark but I can't help feeling like that helpless, injured, listing to one side, maybe even flailing tiny fish around him.

Blinking hard and rapidly, the horrifying images faded with the tinnitus, leaving me with more of just sensations and a few strong clips, "I saw..." What? Your office become a nightmare. "Wait, why am I lying down?"

"Your eyes rolled back, your body convulsed, then dropped to the floor with a nosebleed. I put you on the couch. Now try to remember, it's important." The urgency in his voice sounded more like a worried parent than a boss, so I concentrated a little more.

"Would you believe me if I said your office explode into toothpicks? Glass shattered everywhere. You okay?" I asked with disbelief edging my words as I took in the lack of debris. It had felt so real at the time, but now...

"Yeah, I'm fine," he replied, the worry leaving his voice as he reached over and penned something into a file, my file. "Thanks for the concern, by the way." The corner of his mouth perked in a grin for a moment then disappeared. "Did you experience headaches or anything just prior to the episode?"

"So we're calling it an episode?" Snarky and not my

best foot forward. I know William's trying to help me but, "Sorry. No, nothing like that. I was just talking then, wham! Out like a light." Again with the notes. "What're you writing?"

"Don't worry, it's nothing bad. I just want to keep track of these things. Make sure you don't have an aneurysm or anything."

"Do people actually die in Limbo? Is that a thing? Can that happen?" Was I actually sounding as distressed as my ears were hearing or was that a little voice in my head really that worried? It's hard to tell when you're freaking out about dying after dying.

"Calm down, yes, people can die in Limbo. You're alive but not. It's tough to explain," he said patting my leg reassuringly. But the expression on his face changed as though it were a mask he wears neatly placed specifically to comfort others. William sighed but not the type you'd expect. More like the weight of the afterworld on your shoulders type, and for some reason, it worried me more than I was a few moments ago when I thought the room had exploded. "We exist in something like a parallel time and place to the living world, as best we know. A person can die here and if they do, it's permanent. There is no here or there after that; there's no other place to go except the ground."

Crinkling my forehead I asked, "Am I a zombie?" Smooth - I'm so ashamed. Those words haven't left my lips since a girl and I saw a B-rated zombie flick back in our teens. No wonder she dumped me. But William didn't seem to mind the question. In fact, I think that facade he wears slipped a little further, showing me a less calculated personna and more like there's a real and other person lying just beneath the surface; or maybe I'm reading too much into this. After all, it takes a certain quality and strength to run a place like this and the guy has been here for a long time; and I'd venture a guess you'd have to have a little thicker skin after someone literally yanked your spine out, to do the things he has to do. I still can't get that image out of my head. Yet here he is, trying to comfort the new guy and wrap our heads around the explanations.

"Zombies aren't real per say, you are. You're alive but not the same as before. You get hungry, thirsty, love, hate, work, get tired just like you did in your old life. And like the rest of us, we're waiting to move on."

"To where? Don't you dare say here or there or I'll kick your ass -- so help me!" That got him to grin again. I like doing that to him; making that mask slip. Don't ask me why, it just seems fun in some tormented way. Plus, he doesn't come across as a shark as much, which puts me at ease.

"We don't know." Well, at least he's honest. "There's nothing official that defines here or there. It's just not here in Limbo and not there - the living world, or whatever someone's personal heaven or hell is." Shaking his head, he moved to lay the damp cloth on the edge of his desk. Then I could see it, the light grin pushing the mask back into place. Maybe not as firmly as before, but definitely there. "Some people believe in reincarnation, that has happened before but the paperwork is insufferable," he said rolling his eyes. It was just too much; my brain felt like it was going to catch on fire or explode at any moment. The answers were too generalized, intangible, and having nothing black and white usually makes me leary if not downright paranoid. What is tangible is that I'm dead; no question about it that was an indisputable fact. How I got here is one of those things no one seems to have nailed down yet, just more conjecture and speculation - not black and white which is why I'm here to begin with, I suppose. However, when it comes to someone telling me, I can just sign off on my death and move on to an unknown whatever, bothers me. No one seems to know what here or there is, they just know what it isn't. This philosophical crap is way above my head and I feel like I'm slowly drowning. Cripes, I need a drink.

"You realize this conversation requires a bar and mild intoxication, don't you? Do you have one of those here? A bar, I mean. Any place I can get hammered or a few sheets to the wind. Even a local liquor store will do," I offered, coming across more dour than intended.

"Yeah, I gathered that by the glassy stare you're giving me. Cut work and let's go have a beer or something." Tugging his vest into place he ran a hand through his hair to smooth it down and picked up his coat as we headed toward the door.

"I should get back. Vanessa might miss me. Besides, the way she went on about the coffee this morning was a little intense," I said, fidgeting with edge of my shirt. I have no idea why I do that. It's just, when I get around him, I feel uneasy. There's something off about him and the way he carries himself that reminds me of something in my past but I can't quite put my finger on it. He's never given me reason to doubt or mistrust him so, maybe I'm just being nuts for no reason.

"You're with me, don't worry about her," he said shutting the door behind us. "Besides, take it from me -- the coffee was justified."

Down Cragston for a ways and nestled between two small cinder block stores on the left, as part of what might have once been a strip mall, stood a rather nondescript pub. With no neon sign offering whether it was open or closed, you really couldn't tell; except for the unlocked door admitting willing entry. For what it lacked in color and texture on the outside it earnestly tried making up for on the inside, with two green felt top pool tables on the far left side of the room and a smattering of tall cafe tables with red bar stools here and there. Plugged into the wall stood an old jukebox that I seriously doubted anyone knew how to work and even if they did, I'd bet the music was severely outdated, unrecognizable, and most likely still on vinyl recordings.

Where it not devoid of loud music no one can understand the words to and missing the smell of stale air, cheap perfume, and cigarettes, I'd say it was like any other establishment I'd frequented just before happy hour began.

As for missing out on the technicolor on the exterior, it reflected the same despair for warm bodies on the inside. With the exception of myself and William, there appeared to be no one serving and no one waiting on tables. It was nice.

At least it appeared as though someone once made an attempt at normalcy around here. Kudos to them! For all and all, it was just a simple place with no bouncers to give you a shifty judgmental look when a regular guy like me showed up with a hot date, and apparently there was no cover charge, and that was fine by me. As we approached the bar, stools lined a dark wooden counter as long as the uncrowded room, and chairs remained flipped onto the tables among the cafe setting, resting on their seats. Flipping two stools over at the bar, William reached behind the counter and pulled out two large pint size glasses and drafted us the promised beers.

It was the first time I was able to see myself in a full length mirror. My reflection from behind the bar stared back almost identical to what I remembered looking like, only with tiny white almost invisible scars at my hairline in the front, missing the glasses, and though my skin has always been pale it hadn't looked this pasty since I was born. Otherwise, the spiked short dark hair and soft teddy bear eyes peered back at me like they had for the past twenty-four years, kind of.

"What happened to my glasses? My watch?" I asked staring at my reflection. Not able to help myself, my fingers probed my scratchy jawline; it was still mine but the lingering doubts let my hand fall to to my wrist. My fingers slid of their own accord over the place where a tiny weight once sat as a mild constant reminder of what being early or late use to be. The peppered stubble shadowing my jaw I could handle but it was just weird staring at myself and not having to squint, or my watch to fidget with.

"They tried, I swear they did," William promised, pulling one hand crooked upward to swear by; then, looking over the choices of alcohol at his disposal, he grumbled inaudibly in a frown before settling for his beer. "Props couldn't put everything back together so they patched you the best they could in the time they had. Remarkable how close they came with what was left and a few spare parts in the warehouse." Taking a deep swig he continued, "As for your living space, we couldn't find exact replacements for everything like your furniture and apartment style. Luckily we had some of the stuff in storage. Made it easier to decorate. However, when it comes to human tissue, apparently it's a bitch to match and your eyes were, how did Flo put it? Ah, nothing but a pile of glass and goo. She had to use your driver's license to identify the color and texture. So yes, your eyes did belong to someone else at one time but they're almost identical to your old ones. They're actually better, you won't even miss the glasses after a while."

"But they look so real," I said considering my reflection again. "What'd you mean by finding stuff to replace my apartment? Why couldn't you just pull the original stuff here?"

106

"That's because they are real. They're a donor set. Rarely, but occasionally, we have to raid the morgues or hope someone dies soon with a match for the recipient - whether its eyes, bones, tissue, or organs - we may have to shop around, but we get what we need." William shook his head as he topped off his drink, "Go ahead, try it." Pushing a drink into my hands I lifted it to my lips, wondering temporarily if they were my own and what else might have been replaced. "The original stuff, as you put it, has to stay where it belongs so the living side has continuity. No one misses a piece of furniture from a storeroom or warehouse that was odd or mismarked and suddenly goes missing; but the living miss things from the obvious and that leads to questions, which leads to trouble for us."

"It's cold." Okay, brain - shush, enough out of you.

"Yeah, can't stand warm beer. This is the only bar on this side of town and it never closes so, we don't go bar hopping. We just come in here, get hammered, and crawl home. One of the best reasons we keep the card keys on us." In less than a few seconds he'd downed half his drink and topped it off again. "No one's around so let's talk."

"About what? Furniture? Someone else's eyeballs staring at me from my sockets? The missing money?" We could talk about anything, literally anything. I could have asked him about why there's so much tension between him and Vanessa, or even started this off with how many potential single people are available to date here? Hell, I could have asked about what he did in his prior life or even asked why that strange man stays in the warehouse on Cragston in near total darkness? Nope. I went straight for the money. Brain, meet idiot. Idiot, meet brain.

"Nah - we should chat about more interesting things like life, death, here, there, the rules...the door you two found last night," he said sipping his drink while gazing into the mirror behind the bar. Sneaky. He never had to actually look directly at me to gauge my reactions, truth or lies. The mirror worked just fine.

"What door?" My nervous habit returned - fidgeting where a watch band should be.

"Wanna play that game? Fine. Evelyn, you know her, the little Asian lady with a sparkling attitude, came bouncing in my office first thing this morning thanking me for finally sending her two helpers last night. She described you and Henry to a T. Wanna tell me what's going on?"

"She needed help, so we helped her," I shrugged noncommittally. "No big deal."

"That's not her story. She says she saw you two, as she put it, 'skulking behind a pallet of computers' and that she called you two out. Is she right, or is she lying?" Point blank if not accusatorial. He reminds me less and less of my old boss every minute. I had to find something to preoccupy my fingers and fidget; it was driving me nuts not to have my watch so I did what any kid with their hands caught in the proverbial cookie jar might do--I observed my hands, honestly wondering if the fingers were mine.

"She's sorta right. We found our way there and nothing was making sense. You told me you couldn't afford to pay for equipment, yet there it sits in a warehouse gathering dust." I began looking them over for anything to clue me in, except I didn't have any scars, tattoos, rings, identifiable marks, or even a cut, wart, or blemish that I can recall. Nope. Plain fingers on plain hands. They must be mine.

"Yep." I was expecting a little more from the guy.

"That's it, yep?" Nearly choking on the last swig of beer, I half turned in my seat. The thought of using Limbo as a front or money laundering base was absurd, but I had to know who I was working for, "Jesus cripes! Just tell me, is the money getting funneled into assets? Is that why there's nothing to spend? It's all tied up in stuff sitting in warehouses, like the one on Cragston and Shirley? And what the hell's with that crazy door?" I was on a roll and letting off more steam than intended before he glanced my way, the contemplative shark features effectively shutting me up.

It was a long pause; longer than a few seconds of thinking, even for him. By now I was wondering if he'd lost his train of thought or was just trying to derail the conversation. Staring into the dark liquid swirling at his fingertips, out of the blue came, "Did you know I had a son?"

"Why would I know that?" The words just fell clipped, unchecked at the teeth by my brain. Cheeky bastard, at least give me a moment, "No, sorry."

"S'all right. I didn't even remember I had one until I saw you a few days ago. It just — hit me. Felt like I'd been clocked in the jaw. I'd completely forgotten about him. I guess you look similar to what I used to imagine what he might have turned out like," he shrugged watching the foam slowly dissipate in the glass between his palms. "There was this crystal clear picture of a young man with a baseball cap and glove, throwing a baseball around with me on the front lawn. Couldn't throw to save his life but he loved the game. He hated fishing, camping, the great outdoors — 'too many bugs', he'd say. But I'd always find him in the garage taking stuff apart. He was astute, like you; always wanted to know the mechanics of things. Nothing got by that kid."

"What happened?"

"I died when he was about five or six." Good job jerk. You're not making this better. Sometimes being an introvert sucks. Like now, it just isn't fair to be born with no filter or ability to help others. "Don't be so glum. I have no idea what happened to him or his mother, and that was a long time ago." Chugging the last of his beer, he took a seat on a bar stool, rolling the empty glass between both hands. "Whatever you do, don't even think about going through that door. You can't go back to the way things were. I'm asking you to trust me about the warehouses and

110

money. Just do your job and trust in the system. Your chance will come."

"Yeah well, I'm not feeling all that confident since I got run over in my own home." Crap, that slipped. He didn't even bother looking at the mirror first, nope. Swiveling hard to look me in the eyes, William swallowed hard, shoving the empty mug aside.

"What? When?" he asked alarmed. "Why didn't you report it immediately?"

"The other day when I got back from my walk. Someone bowled me over leaving my apartment. There were two others that'd been following me that were waiting downstairs. We think they took off after whoever it was." Closing his eyes, William took a deep breath, letting it out slowly in thought. "Besides, it was no big deal. It would've meant more paperwork."

"We? You mean you and Henry? Sheesh." Shaking his head, William laid the empty glass on the countertop, spinning it in place. "The suits were my idea. I wanted them to find you and start your case file as soon as they could. Looks like they've got their hands full. That's probably who went after them. I'll have a detail set outside your apartment tonight."

"That's not necessary."

"It's not a question, you're getting protection until we can find out what's going on. Your memories are more vivid and coming back full force, they could do more damage than good." Part shark, part parent. I don't know which is worse, "Don't wanna die again do you? Trust me, it's a one time deal. If you die in Limbo, there's no next time and the paperwork is definitely short." When he says it that way, my core shakes and I don't know if that means I should go with my instincts and run or actually put a little faith in the guy.

"Say I trust you, even a little. You'll have to trust me in return." Not a word from him but those intense eyes were burning right through me. "Starting with no security. I need to feel I'm trusted and can come and go as I please. If anything happens, I promise, I'll come to you first. Deal?" After a lengthy dramatic pause, as if weighing everything we'd talked about against the things he wouldn't say, he stretched out his hand.

"Deal."

Chapter 11

The door to the outside world held open by my chilling fingers, allowed Evelyn to hand the hot containers to Henry's awaiting hands. Beyond lay a kitchen diner devoid of people and lights except for the occasional headlight passing by on the fog-ridden nighttime street.

In a hushed voice, she handed over the containers, "Okay, you two load da cart. I go for next round." Henry questioned nothing and set to work piling on handful after another of dinners into the back of the golf cart. Watching her work the dials, knobs and flipping switches you'd think she was a mad scientist or extreme techie.

"Is this the only door?" It was odd hearing those words fall from Henry's lips. I wondered why I hadn't thought to ask that question since I was the one looking to run away.

"No," Evelyn said as she looked at her grocery list. "Deh many doors scattered across Limbo. Even a few tunnels and gateways but most of dem collapsed aftah second world war. Terrible tragedy. Many not find deh way here. Many lost souls. Damned shame."

"So, what happened?" I asked watching her every move with interest. "You said lost souls as if the Bureau Awakening room isn't the only way in here."

"Yes, and no. People die and come through Bureau because many other doors gone now. No one can come and go as dey please since the King screwed that up. Too many sightings of people in the 70's; too many questions. Too many heartaches and too many problems. Many gates and tunnels crash or blow up in wars. People were trapped, unable to move on and unable to awaken here. Very sad. Now, we have maybe three that work some of the time. Very fickle. Not something I want to put my body through. Evey know this door works. We use this one."

In moments, on the other side of the door, the scenery shifted, wavering and shimmering as if someone had thrown a rock into a pond. Then, in the center, a dark blue pulsing grew. Outward in bands, it stretched until it took up the entire doorway, changing the darkened diner into what seemed to be rain-slicked streets just beyond the stacks of food crates in front of us. The edges of the doorway glowed electric blue as we watched the view on the other side become crystal clear. Stop lights flashed in all four directions at the quiet intersection reflecting on the pavement, the ticking of the lights the only sound next to our breathing. To our right Evelyn crouched her petite body and slid through the opening, staying low to the ground and hugging the brick wall. "Stay here. I'll be back in a few. If someone come by, shut the door. No back talk, no coming through. Unda'stand?" We nodded and watched as she took off quieter than those sneaker shoes should have allowed her to be. Another door down against the brick wall, she dove into a recessed area and disappeared.

Whispering, Henry fidgeted with his long sleeved shirt,"What if she doesn't come back?" I had to admit I hadn't taken that into consideration. He was getting anxious again and I didn't want to follow him down that particular rabbit hole of self-doubt.

"Then we shut the door and you go home; I find William and explain. Simple."

"This isn't that simple." He was going to kill me with his incessant negativity. Thrumming my fingers lightly on the door frame, I knew deep down he was worried and didn't want to be here. I really couldn't blame him. If Evelyn was taking precautions, then it warranted a little more caution on our side.

"What if she's mugged or we witness a heist or something? What if the building catches fire?"

Spinning on him, I ground my teeth, "If you keep this up I'll need to bring a bottle of antacids with me. Cripes! It's going to be fine. Just freakin' relax. She seems to know what she's doing and besides, it looks like she's done this a really long time. Ease up, okay."

Pacing the room, snapping his fingers, Henry nearly jumped when Evelyn bounced through the door handing him four cold containers and me a milkshake. "Hope you like vanilla; all dey had."

Taking it, I thanked her. Sipping the icy treat through the plastic straw was something I didn't know I'd missed until the ice cream headache hit. "How'd you know I needed this?" I said, squinting hard at the pain in my forehead.

"Ha!" her laugh barked forth, "funny guy. Drink slow, you not six anymore." Pulling a key from her pocket she slid it into the console and instructed me to shut the door. Most of the blinking lights went out except a handful and the freestanding door no longer shown light around it. "We done here. You kids go home."

Climbing into her cart, we watched her drive off into the night we stood silently at the guard shack for long moments, the tension nearly palpable. "Why'd you bring me here if it wasn't for the door?" Without turning my head I could tell his eyes were practically boring laser holes through me.

"The facility had armed guards in the day. This place was humming with electricity and people. I didn't come to the front with all that activity. Didn't wanna be seen," he said.

Feeling justifiably prickly, I crossed my arms and let go of a little anxiety that'd been pecking at me, "Just gonna sum this up… we snuck here in the middle of the night when the coast was clear to avoid men with guns who aren't here, found a storage facility filled with electronics that aren't on the books, tons of freaking coffee grounds in canisters just littering the place, and a creepy door to the living world we aren't supposed to go through, except for Evey. Now we're delivery boys and still have no clue why there are massive amounts of money missing in the funds, but we're well fed."

Henry worked his mouth as if it were parched and he was searching for the right words or anything to say. Just let the cogs turn on their own. Let him figure this out for himself. "You didn't tell me about the money." Is he really pouting?

"Well, I'm tellin ya now. Something's off kilt. There's always deposits made to the bank but the amount is always off by thousands, yet the ledgers show they're balanced. Evey seems to be the only one allowed to work this door thing but I never see her take a credit card or cash to pay for the food. Vanessa always seems edgy, maybe because she's in a supervisory position, or there's a lack of coffee in her life. William - I don't know what to think about him. One minute my gut tells me he's a used car salesman or henchman, the next he's picking my sorry ass up off the floor like he cares." Heavy sighing and more weight on my shoulders, just what I needed. More work in the afterlife, "The more we dig around the more questions we come up with."

"We?" his voice raised in question as his hands went absently to his chest, "What's this we? I was happy knowing nothing. Then you pushed me to explore on my own. And after I did, I found this place and wanted to show you because I've been here a really long time and never seen it or those armed people before," he vexed wringing his hands, then pointed to the site. "This street's been vacant for over fifteen years. That building's been empty for almost as long. The electricity has to come from somewhere, the guards had to come from somewhere. The stuff inside had to come from somewhere." The more he explained the more it felt like I was drowning again and couldn't get enough air. This time the sensation changed.

Tightness in the center of my chest blossomed, choking me. The copper stench rose fast as the scenery cracked and replaced by walnut paneling with glass windows. Screams, shouts, panic from all around encompassed my body in a palpable cocoon. Then it hit - something solid. My form moved in slow motion, flying through the air. I had dove for the middle of the room out of panic and instinct a little too late. For a brief moment, for just a split second, the world hit the pause button. Everything stopped except for the loud ringing in my ears and the hard thumping in my chest. I looked around the office. The ledger on my desk was covered in shattered glass and something else. Tentatively tapping the rough surface of the book, my fingers came away smeared and tacky with blood -- my blood. Could I control this one moment this time? It was worth a try.

I hadn't been able to control what happened or how I got here or anything since my arrival, but in this moment, right now, I have a tenuous grip on this version of reality - a memory, if I just concentrate. I should be scared out of my mind realizing whatever happened in that office killed me, and the fear is definitely there, but not for myself; for the others around me. The overhead linear lighting was still on but not moving with the force of the object coming through the wall, as one would expect. The silence grew to a deafening roar, then just as suddenly I was back, lying on the ground being nearly unconscious with my nose bleeding and Henry shaking the crap outta my arm.

"Wake up! Wake up! What the hell happened to you?" The panic in his voice was sufficient enough to bring me around and even though it wasn't necessary, it felt nice to have someone actually worry about me for once. I'd spent most of my life introverted, alone and pushed from one orphanage to another in the system since I was six. Numbers were my only friends and I could always count on them. Numbers are safe and don't lie. It's what made me such a good clerk, to begin with, and land that job at...what the hell was the name of that place? Josephs, Mallin, and Crobbs. That's it, a law firm. "Can ya sit up?"

"I'm fine buddy," I said grinning goofy as my chest relaxed, the feeling of tightness subsiding with the anxiety I'd built up. "Just an episode." I'd done it once, I could do it again, I hoped.

"You don't look fine and I'm betting a milkshake ain't gonna fix this." I wanted to laugh or joke but my body was just too tired to do either. "So, you get a lot of these episode things?"

"It's just what William's calling them. Yeah, this calls for a beer or something heavier. Help me up?"

"Got a li'l something there." Running the back of my hand beneath my nose it came away with a smear of blood. Okay, so how much of that was memory and how much of it was present? I was bleeding in both. Not something I want to think about really.

"It's been doing that lately," I said wiping my hand off on my jeans. "No biggy."

"Are these episode things dangerous? Does this mean you're remembering?" Henry has an issue containing his eagerness or the sparkling effervescence that is him. Even though his concern for me, that little light of hope shone through, I didn't want that being doused by whatever was happening. I also don't want anything bad to happen to him.

"Maybe. It's been pieces and fragments until now." Wobbling to my feet, I sighed leaning on his shoulder for support, "I think it's safe to keep helping Evelyn though. Maybe she knows more about this facility, like, where all these computers and stuff came from. I'll keep looking into the records, see what I can find." Wiping my face again, my hands came away clean but I still subconsciously patted them on my shirt. Looking up the street where she'd disappeared into the darkness, we stared into the nothingness for a moment, "Did you catch that? She called us kids."

Brushing his hair back from his face with one hand, he managed to seem less afraid or worried now. "How old do you think she is?" Shaking my head, I honestly couldn't answer. I have no idea how to gauge time or age in this place. Take William and Vanessa, for example… those two have undoubtedly worked together for a long time, but for how long, no one could say for sure and I could only guess and be wrong. "We're still getting a beer, right?"

Ah, Henry. Easy going and just the friend I needed. "Not a clue; but I'm getting the feeling she can take care of herself. My friend, let me introduce you to the one and only bar in Limbo," I said, draping one arm over his shoulder and mapping the streets from memory.

Chapter 12

Pulling out his card, Henry spoke to it with wonder and reverence in his voice, "Remember this location." The key card glowed light blue then pinned a yellow dot on a partial map of copper lines, just before dimming to a blank surface.

"You really need that?" I asked, suddenly wondering if I had mine on me.

"Yeah, I have memory gaps that leave me in the middle of a street I've been down a hundred times. So this is the bar," he said as we entered through the front door and went straight to the counter, pulling two bar stools down and filling two glass pints from the rack below us. "Wonder why we're the only ones here."

"I suppose it's the same reason you can't find your way around well. People are either too busy with their daily routines and trying to figure out what happened to them, or maybe they don't remember what a bar is; or like you, maybe they just get lost and never find this place." There were a hundred reasons I could think of off the top of my head why no one was here, but not at night. That was always the living's way of celebrating getting off work or looking to hook up for the evening, or blow off steam. I don't even know what day it is let alone the actual time anymore. I feel like I've only been here a couple of days and besides the file in William's office, I had no watch or clock to keep track of it. Catching myself rubbing my wrist, I absently missed that stupid piece of silicon. That one piece of living that was incessant and consistent… time.

"Then that makes us the lucky ones. Cheers!" he said clinking the glass pints softly, pulling me out of my funk.

"Henry, can I ask you a personal question?"

"Shoot," he said relishing the rich delicacy bubbling and foaming around his mouth.

"How did you die?"

Swirling the cool beverage he looked straight ahead into the mirrors lining the wall behind the bar. "Don't really remember," he said, tilting his head a bit. "It's been so long. I gave up trying to figure it out, ya know. I'd been getting closer, I know it. But then whatever evidence I thought I'd found either disappeared or was circumstantial, or so said my case workers."

"Yeah, but do you remember anything?" I pressed.

"I remember waking up in a really large room and being walked down the street to where I work now and introduced to Vanessa. Before that, nothing," he shrugged, "well, except for feelings."

"Feelings? Like love, hate, what?" I grinned.
"Nah, more like...scared. Like I knew what was happening and couldn't stop it." Setting the glass on the

123

counter he spun it in place, not truly seeing the suds, "I know I was lonely, tired, confused and in a world of hurt when I died."

"If you could go back, would you?" I asked peering into the abyss of an amber beer.

"What? And miss having nothing to worry about? I have a roof over my head that resembles my old home, food three times a day, a job I'm not going to get fired from, and now a bar and a friend. What more could I want?" he grinned sardonically. "No, I don't think I miss the living world; but I think you do."

"What makes you say that?" Okay, I suck at hiding emotions and trying to hide in my beer wasn't working. Henry saw right through to my core.

"Because you're fixated on that door to the living side. You're not even looking into your death, as far as I know. Have you even talked to your case handlers yet?" Busted. He knows me better than anyone and yeah, maybe it's why all of my relationships have failed, the lack of being honest with myself.

"Evelyn does it, why can't I?" I snipped.

"Because Evelyn comes back to where she belongs and I'm just guessing here but, you get this glassy-eyed look of longing when you're holding open that door. Like maybe you wanna step through and close it behind you."

124

"Can't lie. I've thought about it."

"But have you thought of the consequences?" he asked as I huffed, rolling my eyes. "Rule No. 1, the dead shall remain dead. You going through to anywhere in the living world can have major repercussions, not just for the living but for us." Draining the remains of his drink, Henry stood, pushing the bar stool back. "Friendly piece of advice — don't do it, don't even think about it. Let the system work for you."

"Yeah, how'd that work out for you? Or William, or Vanessa, or Flo for that matter? Everyone here is stuck, I don't have to be." My tone clipped and sharpened, surprising even me. "I promise I'll at least ask the suits what they've come up with, that sufficient?"

"And if they come up with less than you'd hope for or expect, what? You'll abandon the process and just step through the door willy-nilly?" Henry's face burned bright red, his anger welling but that nice guy tendency suffused the tension; however, the disappointment registered loud and clear, "I thought we were friends," he stared blankly at the door he was walking through, "friends don't jeopardize people or each other just to satisfy their whims."

"Henry," my voice trailed after him but my body didn't move, I remained seated at the bar wondering how I'd gone from best buddy to insulting jackass in under three minutes. New personal record.

Coffee...coffee...coffee...the mantra rang in my ears as

my stomach began to rumble, bringing me out of a restless sleep. Henry's words tumbled over and over as I rolled out of bed and down to the bathroom with sloth motions. Hell, even a slug was going to win a footrace this morning.

He was right, and that's what irked me more than the argument. I hadn't even given the system a fair shot and here I was ready to carelessly sneak off and start a new life anywhere in the world. For Christ's sake, I hadn't even found out how or why I died let alone tried to find real answers. All I have are these memories that come and go whenever I'm stressed and I can't even deal with that. If he'd been one of my ex's, I'd be calling them right now telling them I was sorry and it was all my fault and how I was a jerk and maybe we could do a make-up lunch or have make-up sex or something. Somehow he doesn't seem like the type to consider either of those, so off to work I go.

Files stacked in every which direction lay piled on the corner of my desk promising a daunting task that could keep me busy possibly for eternity. Like clockwork, the interns roll through at high speed with their files and folders running in the wake of Vanessa who's on another rampage about Rule No.3 and making sure everyone knows to refill the coffee maker first thing in the morning. "You'd think they've never had a responsibility in their life," her voice came from beside me unannounced, startling me in my chair. "You're a little jumpy this morning. Everything all right? You look a little pale."

"I'm fine. Just didn't sleep well last night." I said.

"Is it the bed? I know mine sucked for the first couple of months when I got here. I was used to goose down pillows and silk sheets but the closest I got is this satin stuff and a cotton pillow. Can't complain," she said shrugging her files against her. "I was going to ask if you had anything going on this morning but I see the inbox is overflowing," she winced sympathetically. "Poor dearie. New here and already getting buried knee deep. People find out you have someone with talent and suddenly you're the most desired individual. Let me see if there's any people we can assign to you, maybe take a little of the load off."

"That's okay. I'd rather do it myself." No, I wouldn't. What she offered made total sense but I'm in no mood to explain myself, "it's more expedient if I just do it."

"Okay, but if you change your mind, let me know." Vanessa strolled away throwing an apologetic eye back over her shoulder at the monumental stack of work I'd acquired.

The better part of the morning flew by without the need to come up for air. Every transaction led to another question which led to another funnel of money which had questions about where everything was actually going and who was behind it. William had already confided they'd purchased some equipment as assets, which made sense but he wasn't all that forthcoming about the rest of the stuff and why it was being kept in two separate warehouses. And then there's the matter of some of the money being kept in a bank somewhere around here. But it didn't explain the missing tens of hundreds of thousands of dollars coming up missing. Someone's very good at hiding money but not funneling it out. Haven't they heard of laundering? The idea crept into my brain, what if I worked for the police or FBI tracking down criminal money laundering activity? I guess the same could be said if I worked for the mafia or such. But I don't feel like a criminal or a cop, so what does that make me?

"Staring off into space again? My offer to help still stands." Vanessa tapped my shoulder gently, looking over my desk. "Holy cripes you're fast! That stack was at least a foot thick this morning now it's almost gone."

"Like I said, I work better alone," I replied dryly.

"How about some cake or something? I've got three types in my office: vanilla, chocolate, or swirl?" she offered, trying for cheerful.

"I'm not really in the mood. I'd just like to finish these and go home," I sighed. I didn't like disappointing people, especially my boss, but I really did want to just go home. I felt like I'd been on autopilot all morning. I don't even remember doing the work, just shuffling through one file after another until the ledger was complete. There were times, though, when I could have sworn I was working on more than one ledger at a time; I just don't remember what it looked like or where it is other than the dark green one in front of me.

"If you change your mind, my door's open," she said

128

stepping back. The catch in her deep breath hitched, "Get any more of those blue papers lately?" How nonchalant. Almost as if she'd tried to make it organic to the conversation.

"No. Nothing important, just work." Looking over my shoulder, I saw her nod then run her fingers nervously over her files.

"Just asking. I'm here to help ya know. I'm not just some supervisor keeping this place running. I really do want to help you." Hearing her take another deep breath, she tried again, "Have you remembered anything more? Anything I can tell your case handlers for you?"

"Not really. Just plugging along, trying to figure things out. But, I'll let you know if anything changes. Promise," I said crossing my heart with my fingers.

"Well, keep trying. You never know. We have a ninety-seven percent accuracy rate, higher than the postal service," she said proudly, her face lighting up at the statistic. "We've been successful for a very long time. Everyone deserves a home. Just, don't give up."

"I won't," I said as she turned to leave. "Vanessa... thanks, for everything." It was worth the radiating smile she gave, but it still creeps me out how her facial muscles barely move. Then again, I hadn't taken into consideration what she might have gone through to be here. Props may have had to do major reconstructive surgery or extensive repairs to make her look the way she does now. I hadn't even thought of her as someone who'd died. She just appears every morning with her armload of files and runs around keeping the interns running around. Maybe Henry is right about me, all I think about it myself.

Chapter 13

Instead of meeting up with Henry, I ended up alone at the storage room, waiting on Evelyn. When she arrived I explained he wasn't comfortable outside his old job and was going back to that safety net he knew, which technically wasn't a lie. Watching her roll the dials and flip the switches I decided it wasn't going to do any harm to learn how the machine works. Not even batting an eyelash, she gave me a rundown of which dial is for the food and which others control latitude and longitude. The screen above shows the neighborhood where we're going to get the meals and with a flip of the first switch, it shows if it's day or night on the other side. The second switch flipped and the light beneath the door glowed again, charging the connectors to the door. This is how she's able to transport between the worlds, the energy being diverted here, which might explain the large generator in the other room.

"How do you know where it's safe to get the food? Is there a map or something? Do we have a credit card or what?" I asked, the edge in my voice gone from earlier, replaced with excitement.

"Not so dramatic. Know your geography. Dis where Chinese food is very good to get, dis Thai, dis cheeseburger. You can write dem down in your card if need be. Just make sure coast clear before stepping through the door. Going into dat world dangerous." She said sternly. "Too many go through thinking dey run away, start new life and no one know it. Stupid. Everyone death documented. Everyone on internet know what you look like. Had terrible time wit dat Elvis character. He no wanna stay here. He had to have his chicken and mash 'tatoes. Fool! Everyone on planet know what he look like. He show up all over da place. Make mess for everyone here!" she exclaimed, her hands waving dismissal in the air.

"What happened to him? Did he stay out there?"

"No. He big dummy and eat wrong foods again. Die again, same thing here. Buried behind Bureau," she said sternly, then followed it with something in a language I didn't recognize but even so, it sounded an awful lot like a full tilt cussing out. I laughed hard at the thought the King was truly dead and buried in Limbo because he couldn't keep away from fried foods. Oh, how the sensational magazines could have a field day with that. "People like us can no go back to living world. Others can't understand, no place for the dead among da living. Nightmare! I tell you what, I glad I died. I glad I have job and life here."

Not many people would agree to having their lives taken from them, but when I talk to Evelyn, I can't help but wonder, "Mind if I ask how you got here?"

"You mean Limbo? Yeah, I die like everyone else who make it here. But you mean me. In my village, all people massacred by people with big machetes and guns long, long time ago. Friends, family, pets - everyone. Very messy. History repeats self. Can't undo what been done.

Don't want to. Just mean it happens again, only messier. Once enough for me." As if reading my mind, she looked me in the eyes, scanning my face like the page of a well-read book, "No. You no go. You stay with me. Be good li'l boy. Do as Evey say." Patting my hand, almost patronizingly, except she reminded me of what a grandmother would do or say to keep her child from harm, she turned to the door and walked through.

"Evey, how old are you?" I called out as she turned, saluting me with two fingers and a gentle smile full of wrinkles.

"Not nice asking age. You mind store. Be back soon. Maybe I find more vanilla shake for you." I like her more and more every day. Henry was right, again, and isn't even here to gloat about it. It hadn't sunk in fully until Evey said it, I'm dead and there's nothing I could do to undo that fact. I know if I saw a zombie of someone I knew to be dead walking down my street I'd probably beat it to a pulp with a baseball bat, or maybe tear off its limb and bludgeon it to death with the bloody stump, or maybe just run through the town crying like a village loon about an undead invasion. Either way, it doesn't mean I'm giving up on my life on the other side, it just means I've got a lot of work to do researching and learning the rules if I'm gonna find a legit loophole through them.

Knock! Knock! Knock! The rapid succession of my door being pounded on nearly threw me from my bed with alarm. "Knock it off! I'm coming, gimme a sec."

Throwing on a shirt and sweatpants I found on the floor, I looked the door over, no peephole. Who makes a door with no peephole? Turning the knob, I yawned animated as the door opened to view the two suits who'd followed me several days ago. "Oh, you guys. Wondered when our paths would cross." Throwing an odd, unreadable, silent look to one another, the female with her hair tied back in a tight black bun cocked her head to one side.

"Are we intruding?" So official. She sounds like one of those FBI agents from television, just before they flip the badge and push their way into the suspect's house and force them to admit they've been drug smuggling or something. Could I do with a pat down from her? Absolutely. Was I being a prick? Absolutely. Was I about to get my jaw snapped off by a guy three times my size and weight in an identical navy blue suit as hers? I'm thinking, absolutely.

"Nah, come on in." I swallowed against the idea he may have heard my thoughts and averted my eyes. "What can I do for you? Want a seat? Some breakfast? Coffee?"

"Coffee will be fine." The husky gentleman said making his way to sit on my couch. Beside him the lady straightened her jacket and sat nearly straight-backed, their faces stoic.

"It'll be a few minutes, I just got up," I announced rummaging for the cups and throwing together the coffee pot.

"Take your time," he replied. "Nice place you've got here."

"Thanks. Reminisce of home, I suppose." I really hate small talk when I don't know what to say. Wishing they'd arrived maybe twenty minutes from now was obviously not going to happen so I stared blankly at my empty mug as the coffee began to brew oh so slowly. "So, you guys my case workers? Did you catch the guy running from here the other day?"

"He's been dealt with." Just as stoic as before she continued with little to no inflection. If she had been a robot, I'd have at least gotten better responses from it, " Now, Randy, we'd like to discuss our findings this morning and if you agree with them, sign at the bottom of each page and we'll be done." I change my mind. I absolutely don't want a pat down, or anything, from that woman.

Unbuttoning her standard issue official looking 'I don't know what agency you're with' jacket, she came across cold and disconnected, and unfortunately not as kind as I'd hoped. CIA? FBI? Interpol? All the jackets look the same to me, but then again, it could be the late night tv shows inciting that imagery.

"Can I get your names so I don't call you suit one, suit two?" Yeah, I'm burly and prickly without caffeine, deal.

"I'm Sonja, this is Dejesh." Opening her carry case she laid it on the coffee table before her and rummaged through the files, pulling a blue tabbed one second from the top. "One sugar no cream for me, and black for my partner please." Setting the coffees on the table I curled my legs beneath me, perching in the chair across from them, blowing the steam from my mug. "First, we'll need to ask you a few questions, make sure we are where we need to be with the basics; then go over what we've found to help the investigation move forward quickly."

"Sure." What else could I say? They were in my home about to interrogate me and I haven't even had breakfast. "Mind if I say, haven't we met before?" Shooting looks between them they answered simultaneously.

"No." Was that a hesitation or my imagination again? Official people in any capacity bug me. No real reason other than I've seen about a million tv shows and movies where people claim to be from secret government bureau only to find out they're some ridiculously highly trained spy. I know, my imagination is intense but under stressful circumstances it tends to get a little colorful and I can't help it. At least Dejesh had the courtesy to ask, "Why? Do I look familiar or something?" Tapping my mug I put the thought on the back burner.

"Maybe you just have one of those generic looks: male, white, late thirties, weightlifter, ass kicker." Dejesh smiled sitting back but Sonja politely coughed, putting the wet blanket on our conversation.

"Your name on file is Randy. Is that short for something?" I shook my head honestly not remembering if it could have been Randall or something posh like Randolph. "Your expiration was seven days ago?" I nodded yes and answered when she asked if I remembered where I was when I died. "And do you know how and why you expired?"

"Expired. That's such a can of vegetables gone bad turn of phrase. I died, just say that." There she goes again quirking her head as if she were trying to understand what she said wrong.

"Fine. You 'died' at your office downtown. Your toxicology report didn't show any signs of drug abuse, narcotics,any addictions or alcohol in your system at the T.O.D."

Shaking my head, Dejesh clarified, "Time of death." He seems more like the brawn and her the brains of their duo. Wonder when you'd have to use his muscle power in Limbo? Can't be too many ruffians here; everyone's dead.

"However, the injuries you sustained were significant," she continued. "Enough to warrant the entire Props department to put you back together with top speed, accuracy, and at no spared expense, at the Manager's behest. Randy, what do you remember about that day?"

Sagging back against the chair I brought up the memory at will as crystal clear as it had been a few nights ago when I could control it. "I was at my desk, going through the daily and monthly ledgers when people around the office started screaming. I turned from my chair and jumped for the middle of the room. Guess I got clipped or bulldozed by a desk or part of the wall or something weird in an explosion; at least I think it was an explosion of some sort."

"Or something weird? Could you put a better description to weird?" Dejesh repeated setting his drink down.

"Uhm, yeah, something unknown, as in big, heavy, loud, made a crashing noise, squashed me like a bug under a tire - weird."

"Do you remember what was in those ledgers?"

"The Daily log was for current expenditures and asset acquisitions, and the monthly reflected payments and credits. What's with the interest in my job?" He does have one of those faces; one that I can only sense I've seen before. I just can't put my finger on it or pull that vague part of my memory up. Maybe I've seen someone similar to him on one of those Post Office wanted posters, or from a late night infomercial.

"We're just being thorough." Dejesh's answer was a little quick but then again, I'm the paranoid one. I should cut him a little slack because he's just trying to do his job.

"Outstanding," Sonja smiled which seemed like something she was out of practice doing, bringing me out of the momentary reverie. "Looks like your memories are coming back in details. Good." And just as quickly as she smiled, it faded, replaced by a somber slow huff and a professional roll of the shoulders. Once again they shared a quick non-verbal exchange between them.

"Okay, the obvious nonverbal thing you two have going on is kinda scaring me." This is where the anxiety usually kicks in, boosting me into a world of memory control but for some reason, it's not working. I can feel my heart pounding in my chest but not out of control. Then it dawned on me… "I didn't just die, did I? It wasn't some random accident. I was killed by someone intentionally. You know who it is, don't you?"

Chapter 14

"Randy," Dejesh sat forward interlacing his fingers together and relaxing his elbows on his knees, "it just seems too coincidental that you worked for a law firm who was suspected of criminal activity and ended up dead. They've been on our radar and the living FBI's radar for quite a while. To put it blatantly, you're not the first to die suspiciously at their hands." Relief? Anxiety? Anger? What the hell kind of range of emotions should I be feeling? To know that the person who hired me, who gave me my first real job, someone I enjoyed working for, tried and succeeded at murdering me and got away with it? Or did he? Maybe it was that scumbag lackey of a supervisor I had? Maybe he didn't even know about any of this? Or maybe I was just young, naïve, and too involved with my job to notice what was going on around me? Any and all the possibilities raised my hackles.

Clutching the mug a little tighter, I nodded curtly, "So, how do we catch them? Put them in jail or something, use me as bait? I'm in." Again with the nonverbal exchange. Man, that was getting annoying fast.

"We don't. The living FBI are the only ones who can do anything about them. We can only fulfill your file and give you closure, a place to go and move on. The way this case is wrapping up, you might be able to leave for good in a few days or so. Isn't that great?" Dejesh exclaimed. The excitement faded from his voice as the knowing look crossing his face set in, having read mine and others like it time and again. "We know how you must feel but understand, this is how the system works. You need to accept it so you can move on."

The tightness returned full force knocking the wind from my chest. "I don't want closure. I—want—justice," I sputtered, white knuckling the mug.

"Justice or revenge?" Sonja asked, sliding the papers back into the file.

"Is there really a difference? You're nitpicking semantics!" I growled in the back of my throat, the tears I couldn't shed before coming in gasping torrents. "I'm not leaving until I have all the information and make however pay." I can't really swear it on my last breath since that ship's already passed but I can sure as Hell spend the rest of eternity bringing them and their corporation to justice. Unless I sign off on those papers. If I do, it's a done deal.

"Randy, revenge and justice aren't things we can provide here. You need to think about what you're saying and what's best for you." Dejesh folded his hands in front of his chest pleadingly, "If you walk this path, we will know and we'll be forced to rescind your privileges," Dejesh said it as if chastising me and treating me like some six-year-old child. Standing to leave, he buttoned his coat. Just what the Hell did he mean by rescind? Revoke what privileges? Take away my ice cream or key card? Try it and William will hear about it in a heartbeat, you mastodon! "I'm truly sorry you won't be able to bring them to the justice you think they deserve but remember, there's no proof, only allegations at best and speculation it even happened. People have come through Limbo before telling us they remember every little detail down to the minutia, and that's simply impossible, which means they're either lying or desperate or both."

"So you're saying killers never get caught? Criminals just get away with whatever they did and there's no righting wrongs?" Popping up to my feet, I paced in front of the chair, my anxiety ratcheting another unbelievable notch, "What about people like William? Are you telling me he'll be stuck here for the rest of eternity with no closure or justice?" Okay, what was that look? Another one of those silent quick shares between them. They aren't telepaths and I suck at reading people's tell tales and habits.

Sonja ticked her head to one side, "What has William got to do with any of this? What does he think know?"

I stopped pacing long enough to land my hands on my hips; then I saw it, briefly, but it was there. Holy crap. "Nothing." They're fishing. Now what do I do? I can't prove they're not being completely above board with me. It can't be my imagination! What a great time for my paranoia to rear its ugly head. What if I'm wrong and they are playing straight; then there really is nothing I can do. It's time to change the subject before I go off on them, "Let me ask you a question. What if you're wrong?" Hearing the rushing in my head I knew my agitation was leading me to a fist fight I couldn't possibly win. But as least I could puff up my chest and act affronted. I've seen it work for kids who got bullied. Throw out the chest, act tougher than they were, and pray no one called you out on it.

Dejesh was either an accomplished liar or he really was trying to work the situation honestly, "I'm not." Searching my eyes he caught and held my gaze in a cold sympathetic stare, "It's called commonly called Aphantasia and is prevalent from the moment you're brought across the barriers at the Bureau Awakening Room. The condition means it's impossible for people to grasp or retain images and thoughts for any period of time when they expire. It's why everyone's given a key card, so they don't get lost."

"And just who the Hell came up with that load of official bs?" Smacking the mug against my hand, I barely felt its warmth, even as my temper continued to grow. "Who sold you a bill of goods that everyone has some sort of amnesia and can never get their memories back, and if they can they're lying?" Dejesh sighed, swatting Sonja's hands out of the air as she was about to lay into me.

"I got this," he said calmly. "The Manager, of course, and it's not a bill of goods. Believe me, if we thought for one moment there was a shred of hope against these allegations, we'd move on it. But there's not. There never has been and there never will be. We'll do whatever we can to make sure the information is correct in the file and let nature take its course. But in the end, you'll still need to accept the findings and sign off. Don't you want to be happy? Don't you want to get out of this place? Move on to something better?" That did it...

"You're wrong!" I screamed as I threw the coffee mug against the far wall, shattering it in the crash to a thousand pieces. I'd heard more than enough. It was like listening to propaganda and knowing full well what you were being exposed to. Knowing a split second before it's being said, what was going to be said. Asking someone if they wanted to be happy was a way of trying to knock the wind out of the proverbial sail of fury. Knowing full well if they can just get you to relax and unquestioningly go with whatever they tell you, then they have you. Fueled by rage I yelled, "What if I told you when I have one of these episodes, I can control it? What if I told you it stops long enough for me to gain every single detail down to the mud on my shoelaces and the color of a little girl's ribbon in her hair? Am I supposed to believe a lie and just say hey, no problem, I'll let go and move on so you can clear your idiotic books?"

With a deep cleansing breath, Dejesh looked at me, not with hatred or anger but with sadness, "I'd say you're hallucinating or going through post NDE, near-death experience; the after effects of being horrifically killed. People traumatized can sometimes carry that last impression with them. It's how some deal with their own tragedy. They hold on to that last bitter moment and won't let go, so their brain gives them a while to tear it apart and see it for what it really is." Logical and stupid! I really hate this guy.

Gathering their briefcases they moved to the front door, pausing as she turned the handle. "For your sake,"

Sonja said, a little civil, sympathetic and borderline bullying, staring down at the broken mug and coffee on the floor, "you need to find happiness. Accept our findings. Let go and move on — or we'll be forced to deal with you too." The door clicked shut too loudly for the small apartment, muffled only a little by the blood rushing angrily through my veins.

Pacing the room, the furniture paid dearly with my well-placed foot here and there, moving the dilapidated pieces several feet with swift hard kicks. They just came into my home and called me a liar and expect me to roll over and play dead. No pun intended. Scratch that - just accept whatever crap they feel might be fair and say goodbye to my afterlife. They don't even know if you live again, die, or what. Move on? Are they kidding?

Far be it for me to think about revenge and justice. I'm usually a peace loving guy with no clue about heroics and standing up for the little guy, but this time, the little guy is me. And as far as I can tell, these suits are here just to placate those stuck in the afterlife so they can move on and sweep them under the rug and go to the next case.

Ire and the illusion of self-control, the worst combination of forging ahead without a solid plan that's ever been concocted. Going into work seemed useless with everything that had been unloaded in the span of twenty minutes, but with any luck, everything was on paper and left a trail, it was just a matter of finding it to prove a point and solidify my view of this case.

Vanessa's heels tapped across the floor in the wake of the first hour's interns stirring. The percolating coming from across the room accompanied strong whiffs of caffeine in a rich Colombian blend. Oh, how I love the smell and promise of the elixir of the Gods! And obviously so does everyone else this morning. The line began just outside her office and wrapped around to the hall leading to William's office. After a decent fifteen minutes, every eager hand clutched the warm beverage and shuffled with that all too familiar grin across their faces. Limbo may not have everything, but it certainly has a firm understanding of the coffee drinkers addictive needs.

The corner of my desk, buried a foot deep in files again, was the beginning of another day's daunting task. Flipping through as fast as I dared without making any mistakes was child's play. Every nuance that stood out as a possible red flag was one more thing I copied and kept in a separate folder, locked in my bottom desk drawer with a couple of ledgers. If it's evidence they want, that's what they'll get.

"Hey, sweetie." Vanessa's voice seemed to come from nowhere as I slid the key to my desk in my pants pocket. "Oh sorry, didn't mean to startle you. Wow, you're industrious this morning. It's only been five hours and everything looks done. You must've been really good at your last job."

The snarky side of me wanted to say, 'Yeah, too bad the asshole killed me' but without knowing if I could trust her yet, I tested the waters, "Vanessa, I have a personal question, if you don't mind. If you were given the choice to take an opportunity to figure out what happened to end your life, especially if it meant dabbling in possibly bringing justice to a criminal, or finding complete peace by letting go to finally move on without knowing if justice was served, which would you choose?" And when I thought it was impossible for her pupils to increase to the size of saucers, they did. Along with the sudden upwards jut of her chin and brows knitting then releasing in tumultuous thought.

"I guess, I've never actually given it any thought. That's a scary scenario. I mean, my case workers couldn't find out what happened and I couldn't remember more than being a secretary or something. My body was found in the remnants of a fire. There wasn't a lot they could do so mine was held for future research." My gods, the poor woman. I had no idea. But the more I'm around her, the more I'm able to read her expressions, what there is of them. It's always in her eyes. They way they blink hard or soft, dilate or focus intensely, crinkles of laugh lines framing the babydoll look of innocence she can give. And right now she was a little upset but not mad.

"I'm sorry to hear that. I had no idea." I can't help but wonder how many times her dainty shoulders had shrugged like she did just now. Casting off bitterness and replacing it with dignity.

"How long has it been? How long can they keep a file open? Is there a cap?"

"I...don't know. What brought that question on?"

Opening her eyes wide, her expression gained something with her next words, "Oh dearie, have you been remembering? How much do you know?" Panic, anxiety, or hope lay just beneath her breath with each word.

"It's nothing really. My caseworkers strongly suggested I take their recommendation and give up, and let nature take its course."

"That's incredible! You get to leave! I'm so happy to hear that." The bubbling joy practically sprung from her pores like champagne. Maybe she really couldn't help being over the rainbow with happiness for me, but that didn't change my situation or attitude.

"So you'd pick moving on rather than justice?" I asked, deflated at her response.

"Well, yeah. Justice is for the living," she shrugged perkily. "Rule No. 18."

Chapter 15

I really do miss Henry. It's been a week since we parted ways and I haven't heard a peep. My afterlife's starting to mirror my living one pretty accurately and that's just depressing. Get a girlfriend, lose the girlfriend. Get a great job, get killed in said job. Get a best friend, lost friend to insane notions of escape. Get an afterlife that's not so bad, get told let go and move on - someone else needs the space you're occupying. Well, not really but it was implied and it's my pity party; I'll damn well let go when I'm ready, not when some caseworker tells me. Hunched over, staring down at the ledger beneath my quickly moving fingertips, I hadn't noticed the sound of someone dropping off another load of work until shuffling feet nearly tripped on a wastepaper basket a few feet away, alarming me to an upright position. The intern apologized in a whisper more to the basket for kicking it than to me for disrupting my concentration. I should have been offended but sitting in the inbox was another blue note.

Unfolding it, the instructions were in small handwritten letters:

URGENT!

Find Henry. Let no one know you're searching for him. Speak your results to your card when you know directed to me only. - Manager

Past experience with blue notes prompted me not to

wait, or it would just become insistent and whoever the sender is would eventually be forced to come to my desk and kick my ass for not...finding Henry? Why send me? Why not an intern or William or Vanessa for that matter? I'm

not his keeper. On the back, as I folded the note in one hand read:

You're the only one I can trust. Find him!

Sliding the ledger and new notes into the bottom drawer, I locked them away for safekeeping, stowing the little metal key and note in my front jeans pocket. The gathering of evidence for my cases would have to wait. He's probably slobber-faced drunk passed out at that bar. No one's thought to look there first?

"Where ya off to?" Vanessa - she needs a cowbell around her neck. This ability to sneak up behind people in high heels is embarrassing. "Oh sorry, did it again huh."

"Nah, just lost in thought. Think I'm putting in more hours dead than when I was alive." That gave her a sweet chuckle, even if I didn't think it was that funny. "Need to take a break. Stretch my legs, maybe look into some lunch."

"Hey gang," William chimed from somewhere to my right, straightening the pinstripe vest with one hand. "Couldn't help but overhear you're going out for a bit."

"Yeah, looks like it." Not original but when it comes to being in the same room as one or the other of these two, it's manageable, but when it's both it's unnerving. I keep expecting them to pull out daggers and do some kind of mobster gang musical dance number. A dagger jab from her to bongo beats, just missing the midsection. Several small pirouettes from him retaliating with a saxophone barrage of notes, all the while there's dancers in drab clothing snapping their fingers to the tune.

"Oh great, that's just awesome. But, don't be gone too long, William and I want to have a word with you when you get back about a project we think is right up your alley." It wasn't a suggestion so much as a directive. I'm just glad she didn't see the note or key. Gauging from the response she had last time she saw a blue note for me, I'm not ready to get harangued for ditching work or answering a thousand questions I don't have answers to about a stupid note. Neither one is positive, so neither one is wanted, so both of them unfortunately get ignored.

"Sure, I'll be back as soon as I can," I said and with that annoying cheerleader grin, she trotted off. As soon as she closed the door to her office, William turned to me, speaking in a lower tone between us.

"Have you seen Evelyn lately? She hasn't delivered dinner in the past couple of nights." His expression went from happy to concern in under seven seconds.

"No, but I can keep an eye out for her. Tell her you're looking if I find her," I said, shrugging indifference. It wasn't as if I was her babysitter either but it did bother me that she was missing too. Perhaps that's what William was seeing when I coughed, swallowing in my dry throat.

"Yeah, do that for me." Whatever those actors get for daytime drama awards, he should get one. Not being able to tell if someone is actually concerned or fishing for information drives me nuts. That was one of my last job pet peeves. Some mid-level suit who knew nothing about accounting or bookkeeping constantly checking over my shoulder and asking favors. Jerk always knew how to catch me doing ten different things at once so I couldn't yell at him too. Hey, Randy, we'd like you to go to the bank for us, can ya do that? Hey Randy, got this dry cleaning that needs picking up, be a chum and get that for me? Hey, Randy, the boss wants you to pick up an expensive Scotch and hand deliver it to this address. I guess some habits are hard to break because I just can't stop saying yes.

Of the six places I tried, the bar being the first, they all ended up fruitless. No one had seen or heard from him or Evey in at least a couple of days. Not really surprising since most folks around here can't remember their names, where they live, or what they're doing most of the time. But they do remember certain people like Evelyn. According to other residents, she didn't just deliver dinner, she also delivered groceries. And some people were getting mighty cranky their cupboards were empty and so were the coffee mugs. Ya just can't come between a serious caffeine addict and the first brew of the day. It's a Cardinal sin.

Every place I tried came up the same as I began a methodical search up one street and down another, building by building asking everyone what they knew. By the time I reached my street, a tingling began at the back of my neck vibrating as if ants were running a marathon along the hairline. What if someone knows where they're at and they're lying? It could happen. I can't be the only one with a decent memory. But if that's so, how do I know who's lying and who's telling the truth?

Skipping everything on the front and back side of my street, my instincts drove my feet directly to the front gates of the warehouse facility Evey had been working out of at night. Sure enough, Henry had been right. Several guards in uniform with handguns and rifles wearing gas masks patrolled the perimeter. Behind the chain link fence rolled up four large trucks being loaded and unloaded with pallets of equipment simultaneously from the loading bay. Inside every light shown bright, illuminating the already daylit area. Generators hummed drowning out the shouts by a handful of suits giving orders, two of whom I recognize. What're they doing here?

Against my better judgment, I skirted around to the left edge of the complex and waited, watching the bustling activity. As soon as the sun began to set, they all left, quickly wrapping up whatever transaction had been taking place. Sonja and Dejesh met with other suits who had been inside and exchanged envelopes, handshakes, and brief lackadaisical salutes before exiting and disappearing into the falling shadows beginning to stretch across the street.

The trucks rolled out quickly as the military-looking people turned off the lights, closed the doors, and made it look as if no one had been there.

In the quiet and darkness, I went to the spot Henry, and I had cut and wiggled through. I understood now why he'd been a little freaked out. What could warrant having armed military personnel wearing gas masks in Limbo?

Inside the dust had been just as thick as before but was still settling, falling lightly through the air. "What the hell?" New crates and pallets stacked in precise rows replaced what had been there a week prior. Peeling back the shrink wrap, I opened a nondescript cardboard box to find it full of laptops - new ones. Going to the very back row and opening a side box from a pyramid build palletization of boxes, caught me by surprise. Each box I picked up felt and weighed the same so I had to deduce they all carried the same cargo. Poking at tape I pulled it back to reveal not just bills, but stacks and stacks of greenback currency. Slipping a wad of money into the waistband of my jeans, I made sure the box was resealed and buried beneath several others. Mama didn't raise a fool, but she did raise a person who knows when something's not right and is looking at potential evidence. Well, mama wasn't exactly a she. *She* was the state-run orphanage where I got shuffled from place to place my entire childhood from near birth, but at least it taught me some things of value. Presenting proof, tangible and undeniable was what saved my tail from being punished time and again. So slipping a few bills isn't stealing, it's gathering data and doing research. As long as the proverbial cookie jar isn't showing an obvious percentage of cookies missing, and our hands isn't literally in it at the time, we're good.

Sneezing as the dust finished settling around me, I made my way to the room off to the right. Before I could open the door, lightning shots of electrical impulses instead of tingling ran along the back of my neck, instantly my mouth went dry. Stepping into the room with the door, I closed the other behind me. Evelyn hadn't been here, but the door was, for lack of better terms, on and glowing. She would never have left it unattended and on. Something wasn't right. Pulling open the freestanding door, I immediately wished I hadn't. On the other side was a familiar deserted street where the four-way stop lights clicked in the deserted quiet. Yet not far away but tucked among a stack of apple crates, lay the scrunched-up, and definitely dead body, of Henry.

Chapter 16

Henry's eyes never blinked, his chest never heaved, there should have been mist or something from his nostrils or mouth in that humid cold alcove. Placing my fingers at the carotid artery in his neck, I waited patiently for a pulse that never came. Every sign pointed to him being dead, and Evelyn was still missing. Fearing she'd been killed too or I might get caught, I left, closing the door and remembered the sequence Evey had taught me, using my own key to lock the door. It was too much cloak and dagger for my nerves. Somewhere deep down inside I felt at least partially responsible for my friend's death. That little nagging voice in the back of my mind keeps rearing its ugly head telling me if I hadn't been such a prick, if I had just been a true friend when he needed me. If I'd stopped obsessing about leaving and just chilled with the notion and worked the system like everyone has told me, maybe he'd still be around. If I come away from this knowing one thing is that his killers were definitely pushing me up to my limits of what I thought was being an introvert. Maybe they counted on that? I don't know anymore. What I do know is my best friend is dead and I'm partially to blame, I'm nearly friendless in general, being pushed to sign off on my death certificate, and in way over my head and getting pissy.

What I needed was a friend and a drink. I needed to know what the hell was going on. I needed a safe place to be and home wasn't looking too good. Whoever did this obviously stashed the body in a hurry and either didn't know how to operate the door or was about to be found.

Pulling the key card from my pocket, I spoke, "Manager - Found Henry. Meet me at the bar. Now!" I'm going to make them tell me who this jerk is and where to find him! I have no idea who this Manager person is supposed to be but if they're going to send me on errands that can get me killed, by Gods they're going to have to start sticking their necks out further than I have.

If I hadn't been here before, I doubt I could have found my way alone in the dark without the card. Inside, the tables still housed chairs upended and bar stools remained vacant except at the very end where someone sat alone by a lit candle and a tall half empty bottle of Bourbon.

In the dim neon lighting I could make out the embodiment of a familiar suit on a barstool stood leaning against the bar waving me in. I came to sit on the offered stool next to him and poured myself a shot glass of Whiskey, followed by two more before I could even look up. "So, you going to tell me what all this is about?" I asked. William refilled his tumbler and sipped at length before answering.

"First, is he okay?"

"Nope. He's deader than he already was," came my terse reply. I was in no mood for games, politics, or polite conversation.

"That's a shame. I really liked Henry." Throwing back the rest of his drink with a sour expression, William poured himself another and began absently picking at the label. "By the silent huffing and odd glare, I'd say you have a lot on your mind. Start talking."

"How do I know you're not the one who killed him?" I asked observing the bottom of the glass through the drink.

"Now why the hell would I kill one of my own employees?" he asked in an accusatory flash. Taking a deep breath, he let it out slowly. "Sorry. That's gotta be a sore spot with you." Rolling my eyes in disbelief, my shoulder shrugged spontaneously.

"Know where I found him?" I asked, as William shook his head. "On the other side of the door. Someone had stuffed his body in among these crates where no one would see from the road."

"Son of a bitch. We can't leave him there. C'mon," he sighed heavily, standing wobbly to his feet.

"There's more," I said, ditching the shot glass for the half empty bottle instead. "Whadda ya know about the military and new money?" Kneading his brows William blinked hard.

"We don't have a military, we're Limbo," he said squinting, the corner of his mouth quirking then momentarily squirming at the thought.

"Oh yes, you do. And they were there most of the afternoon loading and unloading crates and pallets with suits. Ever see this?" Pulling the cash from my jeans I laid it between us on the countertop. The vein in William's neck pulsed as he stared skeptically at the stack.

"Where'd you find this?" he sneered.

"Same place I found Henry," I said sneering, finally focusing on him. "The food warehouse." The scowl on his face and darkened eyes made me cringe inside. The man can come across debonair and refined, even jovial but this, this is scary - gangster type I'll mess you up where the coroner can't find enough pieces to identify you messed up.

"Show me," he growled.

Flipping the switch and turning the key William watched as the door glowed and I opened it. On the other side, true to my word, laid Henry's remains among the crates.

"Holy cripes," William whispered, nearly choking on his words as he crouched going through the door to kneel next to him. Checking for a pulse as I had, he waved for me to follow. I did as he had and crouched coming through the portal. "Smell that? It's not apples or a decaying body, that's coffee beans." Across the street two silhouettes moved among the shadows cast by the blinking street lights, coming our way. Throwing a warning hand out he signaled for me to stay out of sight and mostly shut the door as I returned to the other side. Peering out I waited, watching from the safety of the warehouse. What if he gets caught? What if they're the killers and he's stuck on the other side? My heart pounded, the blood racing with my poor wracked nerves as the shadows shortened into two distinguishable people.

Walking with purposeful steps, the men came into view, their voices low and conspiratorial. Gods, what the hell are they doing out this late at night? Go home! All I wanted more than anything was for them to not see us and leave; that and not be the killers. I don't think I can handle more drama right now. Crouching as low as he could, William practically looked like a lithe cat ready to pounce as the men came to stand in front of the crates.

The blond one picked at the fraying edge of a crate sitting waist height, toying with the loose wooden lid.

"I'm telling you if he does it again, he's a dead man, no excuses. I'm tired of doing his dirty work." Hopping up, the darker haired shorter man sat on a stack, pulling a cigarette from his coat pocket.

"What? He don't mean to tell ya what to do, he's just different, that's all. Don't be sore." Flicking the lighter he took a long drag, "Besides, it's not like he's the boss or anything. Just tell 'em to take care of his own, you got enough to worry about with the DA breathing down your neck.." Looking around William found a crowbar slid between the crates and soundlessly palmed it as they spoke. Listening, he changed his crouch to defensive in one slick move, still readying to pounce, but in a different way if needed. "Look, if it bothers you that much I'll talk to'em, brother to brother." It was unnerving how much the shorter guy looked and sounded identical to a stereotypical mobster portrayed in those mob movies, the ones with the thick Brooklyn accent, and tough guy bravado. You know them the second they're on the screen, even if you close your eyes you know their voices. The power they represent in delivering their lines; which should have been calming but if you've ever seen one of their mob movies, you know how intimidating those guys can be; and that worried me even more. It wasn't like we were outnumbered but if they pulled guns, it wouldn't matter how many of us there were.

"Yeah?" the blond asked pulling his own coat tighter around him as a shiver ran down his spine. Looking the empty roads over he agreed. Tugging the corner from the crate he'd been messing with, the lid came away. "Hey, look at this," he said pulling a handful of coffee beans up, "who leaves these out in the weather? Don't they know the humidity's gonna pull the oil right outta them? Sheesh, no respect."

"Not our problem. Whoever the schmuck is, he's gonna lose more than a dime on this load," the shorter man laughed. "We'll deal with this in the morning. It's too cold out here." Shivering he jumped down brushing off his clothes. "I tell ya, I hate the coast."

"It's not so bad," the blond said shivering again.

"Damn, this place gives me the creeps. Let's go before your brother comes looking for us and we have to change his mind for him."

"You'd help me take on my brother? For real?" the dark haired man asked incredulously. "I knew you were my best friend but gods." Pacing, he put out the cigarette, smacking his hands together,

"Alright, new plan. We take care of this tonight." Seconds later the sound of something metal clicked. A glint shined up and down the barrel of the gun the man pulled from beneath his coat.

"How do you wanna handle this?" the blond asked.
"Dunno. Haven't decided if I wanna dump the body in the river or bury him in beans," he laughed half-heartedly, "At least we know where to get a shit ton," he said rummaging his hand through the coffee beans around him and pulling his own gun to check the clip. Satisfied with the plan, he made sure the safety was on and slid it back into the waistband of his pants.

"All right, let's do this," the dark haired man said as they turned left out of the alcove, disappearing back into the shadows, their voices trailing softly against the brick walls.

Slumping to the ground, William wiped the visible sweat from his forehead, signaling me to open the door.

"What the hell?" I whispered frantically, swinging it wide. "Did we just witness a hit being planned?"

"Appears so. That, or a coup' d'etat." Taking long steadying breaths with his hands shaking, he laid the crowbar on the ground. "Don't worry, I don't think they'll be back tonight. Might see'em in the future, or that brother guy though." Reassurances aside, I was positive if we stayed much longer we were going to end up like Henry. Suddenly, Rule 16 and Rule 4 were becoming more important for me to remember: you shouldn't interact with the living and don't leave the door open, close it behind you. Who else knew these rules that didn't belong in Limbo?

"Great, now can we go?" The wide eyed maniacal look I was giving should have been a dead giveaway that our safety should be first, but knowing William, he'd want answers, not loose ends; the man's a lot more like me than I care for sometimes. And sometimes I wish I could just leave those loose ends alone.

"We can't leave yet," he was going all detective on me and I couldn't blame him. "We need to figure this out. Collect whatever evidence we can."

"Then let me start this off by asking why? I mean, if Henry's dead why hide him among crates filled with beans on this side? He's already dead. Why not bury him on the Limbo side?" I asked, watching for the possible assassins to come back.

"Simple. Too obvious. A fresh grave makes people ask questions. They wanted to hide his scent until they can come back and dispose of the body permanently. Probably in the harbor. Drug lords used to do the same thing to cover the smell of products like cocaine being brought into the country. It'd fool the canines and police by hiding the aroma," he explained.

"Why do you know this?" I quirked, as he began rifling through Henry's pockets.

"Why don't you?" he snapped back. Wiping a hand across his face he sighed, "I watched a lot of late-night educational television back in the day. Someone's going through a lot of trouble to hide him but they don't know how to fully utilize the machine. They don't appear to have a key and his keycard is missing."

"So, Evelyn may still be alive? They need her to operate the machine to get rid of the body and evidence, and without her..." The hope welled behind my chest, thumping in time with my heart.

"They can't finish the job. Nice deduction by the way. You'd make a helluva detective," he said pointing to Henry's legs. "We can't leave him here. We'll have to carry him back."

"But if whoever killed him comes back, won't they know he's been moved and they'll change their pattern?"

"But if whoever killed him comes back, won't they know he's been moved and they'll change their pattern?"

"You really are good at this," he grinned. "Okay, then we leave him here, for now. Those other guys could come back and find more than they bargained for; especially if they plan on using these beans to cover their tracks and hide the brother's body." Closing his eyes, William let loose a heavy sigh, "Show me the rest of what you found."

Out in the warehouse, the boxes and crates stood as a silent testament to whatever crime was being committed right under his nose. The strong smell of coffee sticking with our every movement.

"They even respray the warehouse when they were done with fresh dust to literally cover their tracks," I explained, pulling back the shrink-wrapped laptops. "Henry brought me here a while back through a side entry. He told me then about the armed guards at the front and when I came back looking for him, I saw something I don't think he knew. A handful of suits, caseworkers here working side by side with these guys taking what looked like bribes. That's not all, Sonja and Dejesh were here too."

"How'd you stay hidden?" he asked dubiously.

"I turned the corner at the end of my street and stayed behind the fences and buildings out of sight. That may be what Evelyn's doing. We need to find her before they do," I said.

"Agreed. But don't tell anyone about any of this.

Especially your caseworkers. Keep your distance from them whenever you can and when you can't, you come to me." Alternately rubbing his hands slowly, that dangerous shark look came back into his eyes, "I have some research to do. Think you'll be okay for a while? Do you want to stay home, lie low?"

"I think it'll be better if I show up to the office, probably safer that way. Then again, last time I thought that something crashed through a wall and tore me to pieces on purpose."

"That won't happen again, I promise. On that note, I hate to ask like this but, have you remembered anything more about your own case?" he asked.

"Yeah, lots. Too much really." And there it was, I just couldn't keep my mouth shut, "When I had my last episode I was able to pause it, see all the details down to minutia. When I told Sonja and Dejesh they reduced it down to some kind of post-traumatic crap and dismissed it entirely. They suggested strongly that I take their opinion, sign off on the paperwork, and let nature take its course - or else." Kicking my toe at the ground felt better as the tiny rocks scattered in every direction under my low-level ire.

"Or else? Or else what? Did they threaten you?"

"Kind of. Sonja did actually. She made it seem like she's dealt with others in a more, how should I put this - professional downsizing term before. I don't know what she meant by that but it definitely pissed me off." The shark features he has were not happy ones. The man was becoming predatory and protective. I can't say it was a great feeling because frankly, I was still a small fish swimming in a much bigger ocean than I was used to. And this ocean was becoming more polluted and cramped with whatever was going on, by the minute.

"Stay away from them for now on. I mean it! Until we get all this straightened out, you're to carry your key card on you at all times. I don't want you going missing too," he said fidgeting, running his hand down the sides of a pallet of small boxes with oily sides, then pulling his fingers away with a quick smell. Kicking at more rocks I watched him tapping his fingers atop the small boxes in thought until he stormed out of the building, heading across town almost at a jog.

The pub was still empty but this time instead of cozying up to the bar, William grabbed his favorite bottle and uncorked it, taking a long swig before setting it in front of him on the bar. Joining him, I sat a couple of seats down, giving him some personal space to think, but I also needed a few answers of my own, "William, I asked Dejesh who told him people should just roll over and accept their death, even if they've been wronged. I thought he was full of crap but he said it was the living FBI's job not theirs to put away criminals and that the Manager told him to say those things. Is that what you said? Are you the Manager?"

"I didn't," he growled again from the back of his

throat, more menacing. "And yes, I'm the Manager. Satisfied?" I was, but he wasn't, and I wasn't about to pursue it. By the furrowing of his brows, I could tell the used-car salesman act was just swallowed whole by the shark in front of me. "These guys have been running around unchecked for way too long. Apparently they've been pushing people through the system, convincing them to simply let go, that nothing can be done to save them or bring them justice on this side." A harsh edge crept into his voice, "The line gets drawn here. No more of this bullshit. They wanna see what we're capable of, then we'll show them what we can do." Tipping the bottle of Bourbon back, William took a long deep swig, relishing the burning taste with a devilish upturn of his mouth.

Chapter 17

Clip clop, clip clop, clip, clip. I could hear her before I saw her, "I thought you were coming back from your walk yesterday? We were supposed to have a meeting with William, remember?" Vanessa's voice grated with micromanagement irritation after I'd heard her coming a mile away with those shoes.

"Actually, I ran into him earlier and we chatted a bit. He might take that meeting today if you're still available though." Always leave them believing they're in control, even when they're not, is what I always say. "How about now?"

"Oh," fidgeting was never a lovely expression even on someone as manicured as Vanessa, "I suppose we could. Just let me check with him first. I'll be right back."

"Great. I'll just grab a pen and paper and wait here for a hand signal or something," I said, grinning. As her heels clip-clopped off down the hall, I threw the files I'd been working on into the bottom drawer and locked it, just in time. Leaning out into the hallway she gave me the waving signal for me to join them back in his office.

"Good morning Randy," William needs one of those awards, I swear it! The man can play the part convincingly, right before your eyes without even a hint of what went down yesterday. "I'm glad you two reminded me, I'd completely forgotten. We've been so utterly swamped up to our navels and earlobes with new interns and work, right Vanessa?" Nodding she simply agreed and took the comfortable seat I normally sat in. Pulling up another chair, I set myself at an angle to put them both in my vision equally. "I apologize for the inconvenience, so let's get to it. Vanessa, the proposal, you have the floor." It was like crowning the high school head cheerleader with a tiara the way her cheeks flushed pink and her eyes twinkled.

"Right. We have a backlog of files dating back nearly a hundred years in an archive area of the warehouse and we'd like you to consider updating them, making sure they're in order and nothing's missing. You know, the white glove fine tooth once over. I actually put your name in the hat for this since I've seen how fast you work on a day to day hustle. The intern's heads are on a swivel when they walk by your desk with jealousy. So many are waiting to get on the list."

"What list?" I blinked, confused.

"The list of people who want to be mentored or tutored by you, of course. The list is posted in the break room next to the coffee pot. I didn't think you'd mind helping bring these people up to speed and have them work at least at half the speed you do." How can someone's eyebrows not move? I can tell she's trying to pull them up by her other facial muscles but it's just not happening.

"No, that's fine. I can try to schedule a little extra time for them. Is there a cap or limit on when you want the project complete?" I asked.

"No, it's just an extracurricular activity we thought you might enjoy, and we'd benefit by getting everything up to date," William said interlacing his fingers, gesturing open palmed.

"Sure, as soon as I finish reading the manual you gave me on day one, I'll get right to that list and manage the daily workflow and find a few minutes here and there to work on that too. No problem," I said with a touch of sarcasm dripping in my voice.

"If it's too much, you can say no. It's not a directive, just a thought we wanted to run by you," William said, but it was more what he wasn't saying. I've been around him long enough to pick up little things like when his eye go dark, he's angry as hell, and when he's asking you for a favor without telling you he needs one quietly from you for a reason - like now.

"I'll find the time." My weary grin hadn't convinced anyone in the room, especially me.

"Maybe I can help you a bit," he offered. "Show me how to catch up to your speed and we can get through it faster."

"Oh, I don't think that'll be necessary," Vanessa blurted. "I mean, you've got so much on your plate now, why overload it?"

"Because of who I am - and I can," he said confidently, smoothing a hand over his vest. The message being conveyed that he was in charge was not in dispute, but rather was she getting the message clear? "Don't worry your pretty little head. It's not like any of my work will fall on you. You're in the clear." Was that really relief I saw in her shoulders or condescension? I'm leaning towards she's getting pissed off.

"Okay then," she said, her smile not fooling anyone as well, "I'll show him where they are and he can start whenever." Anyone else feeling the tension like a noose, or is it just me?

The last time I'd been to the warehouse on Cragston Street was to retrieve Prop's inventory in the spooky darkness, alone, with a creepy old timer who barely spoke two words. This time wasn't much different except I had Vanessa with me.

Inside still seemed like a huge city of pallets thrown into the dark ages with the humming of a forklift going back and forth, up and down unseen aisles for what looked like three city blocks away; the headlamp on the old timer's helmet nothing more than a bright dot indicating his possible whereabouts.

"You've been unusually quiet," I said, watching her read something on her keycard then the tag on a crate.

"Sorry, I'm just really focused right now." Throwing a quick grin my way, she continued to fuss and fidget over finding the right row. "Damn it! I can never figure out

Gus's labeling."

"So the grumpy old guy's name is Gus? Good to know," I said. "Why don't you tell me what number we're looking for and maybe I can help?"

"It's back here somewhere. 14M27P-5xP." Stamping her foot in frustration she heard the same crack I did, "Ohh, and there goes my shoe. I just can't win today," she whined resignedly.

"Maybe we can fix it." Now, why on earth would I tell someone I can fix their shoe when I know nothing about it? "We can swing by Props, grab a little glue and putty and be good as new."

"That's so sweet. I didn't know you knew how to fix things. What else can you fix?" she asked taking off her shoes.

"Maybe only shoes. I can't fix people." Seriously? What the hell? I'm not an extrovert. This is why I can't keep a girlfriend, I don't know when I should open my mouth to communicate like a normal person, and other times I can't seem to keep my big mouth shut. "Seems you and William are either working separately and keep your distances or you're collaborating and keeping each other at arm's length. It's none of my business but, I'm pretty sure that's not how business partners are supposed to work."

"You picked up on that huh?" she sighed. "He's a nice guy, decent boss - really."

"But...?"

"But, and you can't tell anyone I said this… he's a bit weird. I don't think I trust him completely," she said, nibbling her bottom lip a little conspiratorially.

"What makes you say that?" I asked, checking the markings on the walls I hadn't noticed before. Tapping her on the shoulder I pointed off in another direction and she followed.

"I can't pinpoint it. He's secretive, aloof, macho. Puts on this air like he did back there with the whole 'I am who I am' thing. Drives me nuts," she said with a huff shaking her head. "I swear, one of these days he's going to find my good shoe up his..."

"Found it," I remarked. "There are numbers and letters on the walls. So it's 14 over in aisle M, 27 down in P and there's more than one so maybe 5 is the number of pallets." The next second was shared with the fastest kiss on my cheek I'd ever had.

"You're brilliant!" she exclaimed, hopping up and down.

"Hey Vanessa, why didn't we just use our cards in here to find it?" I asked.

"They aren't that specific. They can get you to a general location but not with pinpoint accuracy. Like if I ask it where Props is, it'll show me a map of where I am and how to get there but not anything specific. I'd have to find the door on my own," she explained, opening the first two boxes.

"These are not in the best shape but if you need new files or anything, let me know. I have a whole stash of them; well, somewhere." Note to self, just get what you need from the other storage facility and don't ask where she gets her stash from.

"So we're just refreshing the files, making sure nothing's missing, names, dates, places?"

"Actually, I'd like you to look into a more specific name and death," she said lowering her voice,

"mine."

"Isn't yours on file in William's office?" I asked reading the names across the tops.

"One of them is but I don't think it's the right one. I think," she paused taking a deep breath, "I shouldn't be telling you this but I think my caseworkers screwed up my file and maybe, just maybe they put the one they wanted us to see in his office and filed the original back here somewhere. It'd be a huge favor to me if you found it. I need it. I need closure."

"I see," I said leaning back against a large crate behind me. "You'd like to see if anything was missed because of what I said yesterday. That my caseworkers are lining me up for a quick exit."

Twisting her fingers she pleaded unabashed, "Most everyone that comes through here leaves and gets a 'here' or 'there' to go to. I've been stuck for years and it's eating me alive. What if I'm not supposed to be here? What if I'm still here by mistake? I wanna leave. Is that so bad? Is that so wrong?" she whined pouting. I really wanted to tell her it seemed like all you had to do was give up, not care anymore, and let go and you'd go to wherever you're supposed to go or be. But that helpless puppy dog look was breaking my heart.

"I'll do what I can on the down low. No one else will know, I promise." Yet another peck on the cheek. I'm getting more affection in the afterlife than I did when I was alive.

Chapter 18

Pulling the keycard out to my apartment I paused on the top steps in mid-stride. Only a few feet away came the sound of the console table by the door inside being tripped into and the glass bowl crashing to the floor, followed by an array of colorful language you wouldn't hear on anything other than cable television. As the doorknob turned, my feet carried me back down the stairs quickly.

Hiding beneath the stairwell in a small dark closet of brooms, mops, and chemicals I could hear their footsteps creaking above my head. What felt like dirt fell through the cracks landing in my hair and sprinkling across my face as the familiar images of those dark suits crept closer. Across the back of my hands and scalp felt itchy, tingly - alive. No time for that. Pushing the insistent niggling ideas forming into undead spiders crawling across my skin, waiting to taste me brought serious panic to my chest. They don't exist, it's your late night tv brainlessness over thinking. I haven't seen any spiders so they don't exist here, like animals. William said there were none. Didn't he? Listening hard I forced my sweaty palms to remain on the doorknob, holding it barred closed by sheer will. I knew though, if they really wanted to get to me, all they'd have to do was try and I'd have no strength to hold off the two of them.

"He'll be back," Sonja's resonance vibrated in my chest leaving only the feeling of danger when she spoke, "and so will we."

Sweat trickled down my back mimicking tons of tiny eight-legged undead things I didn't want to think about. Damn, they were taking their sweet time leaving. "What if we just wait here for him? Go over the finality of the paperwork and make sure he signs tonight?"

"Hey yeah," she said sarcastically, "and maybe we'll find that old Asian bitty before they do, and Henry's key will magically appear. While we're at it, I'll just whip up some special cookies and he'll be overjoyed to sign his afterlife away. What brilliance. He's not going to sign or give in until we do what we came to do."

"It doesn't have to be that way," Dejesh's warning in his voice burrowed an even deeper sorrow into my soul. "I can talk to him, he'll understand. You remember what it was like when you got here and so do I. He has the right to know everything and seek justice."

"What? You're on his side now?" Sonja huffed, "You're getting soft in your old age. Think about what you're saying. He doesn't need to know shit about anything. He needs to let go, sign off and go the hell away. That's what we're paid for." Between the cracks of the door could be seen Dejesh's jacket adjusting across his shoulders and cuffs.

"That's not what we signed up for and you know it," he said in a warning breath. "We're FBI, dead or alive, it's what we do, it's who we are, and this isn't justice."

"No, this is money. This is keeping the books clean. This is doing what needs to be done for the sake of us all, living and dead," she gritted poking him in the chest. "Now get your head on straight. We were told to get him and the Manager out of the way or gone for good in twenty-four hours." Placing his hands on his hips, Dejesh stood for what felt like an eternity before opening the front door to the building.

"Sonny - what if we don't? What if we can't get them both to move on, sign the papers?" he asked but without a pause, she answered.

"Then we dispose of them both. Clean and simple. And if you're not with me on this, you'll end up like Henry. Got it?" The insufferable pause was killing me, almost literally with little to no fresh air and my hands aching from the constant strain of holding on to the door. Dread filled me in a wave of nausea hearing her callous remarks. Finally, he huffed and gave in, his head nodding.

"I hope you know what you're doing," he said with a pang of distress, the click alerting me they'd left. William.

Pulling my keycard, I whispered, my voice and hands shaking, "Where is William?" but the card remained blank. "I don't have time for this. Take me to William." The surface copper line rose and beneath it showed a portion of the map, barely visible in the poor lighting. In seconds the copper line formed leading from my apartments to Props. Then a thought occurred: "Take me to Evelyn." The copper line remained in place. "Okay, how about show me where Evelyn is located." Again it remained unmoving. "Fine. Show me where Sonja and Dejesh are located." The city map focused on my apartment complex glowing yellow, the copper line disappearing. "Crap."

Now I wish this all had been a dream. Something I could wake up from, let all the bad things and impossible irrational thoughts just go away. Part of me still isn't convinced I'm not on my couch about to roll off onto the floor with an amazing headache from too much alcohol. But the other ninety-nine percent knows for a fact I'm not hallucinating, under the influence of drugs or alcohol, or even asleep in the back row of a B rated movie I've seen a hundred times. No, that logical part knows I'm living in the afterlife and if I don't do something to stop whatever is going on, more bodies are going to pile up beneath those apple crates in the alcove.

The hall I practically ran down, lined in that hideous 1970's burnt orange and gold trim, disappeared beneath my feet. Humming with occasionally flickering lights, it cast my thin bizarre shadow ahead of me as I hugged the wall, shrugging off my imaginary hitchhikers with wild swatting arms.

Making my way quickly toward the exit sign at the other end felt like miles away instead of a hundred feet. But the thought of Dejesh and Sonja possibly trailing me, catching me, I know I'm not athletically built, and I wasn't in the best shape of my life when I died, but the thought that they'd disposed of Henry without hesitating, and now wanted William dead, well let's just say I'm motivated.

My lungs heaved, burning in every cell and membrane in gasping breaths. Not bothering to knock, I slipped into Props, checking the keycard to see if Sonja and Dejesh were still babysitting an empty apartment, but they weren't. The card displayed them walking the streets methodically. "Shit."

"Who's there?" Flo's voice echoed in the dim moonlit room. Diffused light filtered through grimy tall windows casting everything into light blue tinged secrecy, the darkness barely held at bay. "I'm tellin' you now, if ya don't come clean I'll find ya, and do things no Props agent should be able to...and get away with it."

"Flo, it's me, Randy." Stepping from the doorway she jogged up to me, hugging me tightly.

"Oh dear lord, you're okay. Come on." Tugging my hand she led me through a maze of things I don't think I could describe except I've seen them in old movie reruns on tv. Some of it looked like mannequin parts and old jugs wisping heavily from the rims. I barely had time to take in the oddities of different types of clay and molding plastics on benches to drums of what could only be formaldehyde by the smell and paint. Lots of paint and sewing needles. "He's here," she announced coming to an abrupt halt in front of a picnic table where Artemus, Mortimer, William and Evelyn sat.

Jumping to his feet, Arty grabbed my hand, shaking it vigorously. "I remember you," he said, smiling wide and toothy. "Some kid, didn't I tell ya."

"Eh, leave the kid be. He looks like he's run a marathon," Morty said scooting over. "Sit down before ya fall down." Catching my breath, I sat wondering all the while if this was such a good idea.

"Holy crap, you look like hell. What happened?" William asked, propping his elbows on the table, lacing his fingers in front of him.

"Dejesh and Sonja were waiting for me at the apartment. I barely had time to hide, but it seems they're up to their necks in whatever is going on and...I'm certain they're the ones who killed Henry," I sighed.

"Did they say that?" William asked shooting a look toward Evey then back to me.

"Yeah, I think Sonja did it. If nothing else, they can't find Henry's key or Evey here. But there's something else, they're out to, and I'm putting this in air quotes, 'convince', you and me to come to their terms and sign off on our afterlives. They want us out of the way, tonight." After several moments of silence, William nodded softly.

"That's a shame," he said almost quietly. Evey continued staring at some blank spot on the table, nodding much the same. "Were any military with them?"

"No. I didn't see anyone else, but then again, I didn't go inside. I just hid and ran when they weren't looking."

"And Vanessa? Have you seen her?" he asked.

"No. Is she in trouble too? Do I need to go find her?" my anxiety ratcheted at the thought someone I was kinda liking and sorta trusted might be in the mix and not know it.

"Good enough. I've got it from here." Standing from the bench he patted Evey on the shoulder,

"It's time. Flo, Mort, Art - you know what to do." Buttoning the top two buttons on his coat he ran a hand smoothing down his vest, "Randy, you can sit this one out. You've done well." Holding out a hand he waited expectantly, "Give me your keycard, go to my office, lock the door, and stay out of sight."

"What? No! Are you nuts?" my voice exclaimed without thinking first. My insides turned at the thought he was benching me, just when things were getting interesting.

Chapter 19

"This has gotten too dangerous, it's for your own good. They can't track you if you don't have your card on you. It's only a matter of time before they find all of us and we don't know how many agents are on their side. My office is reinforced. You'll be safe there."

"Hate to break it to you but no place is safe if they bring military buddies with guns and a large enough truck to..." Searing high pitched frequencies bounced in my head, cutting off whatever I was saying. Focusing on the pain shooting through my body, the room became my old office.

This time, I was ready.

Behind me the walls began to crack, bursting in slow motion, throwing splinters and planks of wood in every direction as I concentrated. Glass fragmented in every shape, glistening like diamonds, sparkling in the air. The room became still as I moved through it cautiously. Every second was an eternity to put under the microscope.

Starting with my desk I sat in my chair pulling it up to a more comfortable height. Ledgers of every color stacked neatly across the front with papers, bookmarks, and pens holding places to refer back. The calendar blotter below my hands showed times and dates highlighted yellow for Tuesday laundry dry cleaning and Thursday bank runs like clockwork. Friday had the note: meeting with manager penciled in but otherwise, nothing stood out.

Pushing the corners I spun it in place, watching papers ruffle in its breeze and a key slide out of a hidden pocket from the back. Picking it up I looked it over, the familiarity of the weight, size, and texture was just like the one I own now. By instinct I reached down to the left-hand drawer, using the key to open it. Inside sat six black ledgers I pulled and placed before me.

Rifling through I knew what I was looking at...motive. Whoever my boss was, he was laundering money for big movers and shakers across the globe and I was just some kid who got unlucky enough to figure it out, and dumb enough to keep track.

Picking up the books, I held them tight against my chest as if they were a shield. Standing from the chair I pushed it back, looking the room over again. There had been people standing no more than ten feet from me talking about inane stuff most people do at work: baby showers, upcoming gift giving to someone they don't like, another person caught cheating on their date and getting dumped by text message. Everyone had somewhere else to be, except the scumbag standing in the hall, protected by a bulletproof glass door. The jerk who kept sending me on these ridiculous errands to the bank and laundry for him, stood behind those doors - safe.

How long could I keep this up? My head was throbbing, blood seeped from my nose trickling across my lips. Just a little longer. I already knew why, and had a pretty good idea who ordered me dead, but I had to know what it was that killed me.

Walking to the wall, still crackling in slow motion, I let go of the control for a moment, letting time resume a normal pace. Holding my chest, I suddenly couldn't breathe. Pushing my mental limits I tried for the control and barely grasped it in time to see the front wheel and partial hood of a large vehicle coming through.

Inspecting it with my hand I could feel the heat from the engine, the tires moving beneath my fingertips as their tread ate away through the wall. As fascinating as it was to finally know what hit me, it was more interesting to catch who was driving; someone in camouflage with a gas mask.

I'd seen this somewhere before. Staring disbelieving at the man behind the wheel who took my life on someone's orders seemed more anticlimactic than informative. Now I had a how and why, but he wasn't alone. Next to him, barely visible in the bleak morning rain, sat someone scrunched into the darkened recessed corner of the cab. Someone partially obscured by the angle he sat and impact the vehicle made. Clutching to the books, my jaw tightened. Dejesh.

I remembered.

"We gotta stop meeting like this," I said wearily, blinking as my eyes adjusted to the lantern casting orange light in Mortimer's hands.

"He's alive," Arty whispered, clapping his hands

enthusiastically to his own chest.

Putting a hand beneath my head and shoulder, William assisted me upright, "That one seemed pretty intense. You were out for a while, convulsed a bit, then went still. Had me worried. You all right now?" The concern creasing his brows matched the tone in his voice, like a parent might use. Once a father, always a father.

"Yeah, I'm good, I think." Sitting up, my legs swung across the table, dangling off the end.

"Trippy to say the least."

"Trippy?" William asked.

"Yeah, you know all psychedelic, colorful," Mortimer said with a knowing grin, "or, not. How would I know?" Shoving his hands in his pockets, and coughing uncomfortably, and turned away to stand by the wall.

"Actually, more like I know almost every detail of my death, including why and how and most important, I suspect who," I said looking down to the floor then up to William who seemed both confused and happy at the same time. "But we should swing back around to Mortimer's explanation, I'm finding it intriguing."

"Sixties love child. 'Nuf said." Mortimer grinned, throwing a quick V-shaped peace symbol with his fingers.

"Looks like you will be leaving us after all," William smiled sadly. I wasn't buying it. Not for one second.

"Nope. These bastards need to pay, one way or another. My times not up 'til I say so." Hopping down my legs gave out from beneath me. Between Flo and William catching my rear from hitting the ground and pulling me back to take a seat, I knew I'd overextended my expectations and reality.

"I hate to ask this now but," William frowned kneeling next to me, "what details can you tell me about your death?" It was like everyone was living vicariously through me the way they stared expectantly, hanging on to each word for hope or something tangible.

"I was able to pause everything like before. Interact with objects, people," I said thinking back to moments ago. "To feel what I can only describe as the pain I was experiencing at the moment of impact when a military guy ran me over. Like the one I saw here, at the warehouse." Suddenly I found William's hand squeezing my own fear and visible anger coming off him in waves.

"What?" It was an unmistakable tone I'd heard before. The look of a dangerous man stared back at me through enlarged pupils, the crystal blue iris barely visible. "A military person from Limbo drove through the wall where you worked on orders to kill you?"

"Did I mention he was wearing a gas mask?"

"What the hell's going on here?" he ground through

his teeth, using the table to stand next to me.

"I thought your case file was going to be open and closed. A week max. Your file said you were eidetic. Then you started remembering details so fast, so soon, it gave us hope." Pacing he rolled his neck with tension, "I didn't suspect anything when Dejesh and Sonja volunteered to be your caseworkers. I'm sorry I put you in the middle of all this."

"William, maybe you oughta tell him everything, or at least what we know?" Flo suggested wringing her hands. "Better armed with knowledge than dead with no clue."

Crossing his arms, William took deep breaths weighing the possibilities. The crinkles around his eyes showing more tension than a manager should, but enough that a friend would, "You're right."

"Hold on," I said waving him to calm down. "What do you mean hope? I'm here like all of you, stuck until my case file is complete. Aren't I?" But as William continued pacing and everyone suddenly got that 'don't look at me' look, I started to get a funny feeling. One that I hadn't suspected from these, of all people. "Just tell me what I'm doing here and what you know." I have no right to demand anything from these people. They brought me across when they didn't have to. They put me back together and gave me an afterlife, also something they didn't have to do. But somehow I'm a pawn in this little scenario and I have no idea what game we're playing. At least give me the freaking rule book! Reading my mind or at least my disappointed expression, he took a long look around the room then focused on me.

"You're here not just because of what happened to you but why and how. That photographic memory of yours is what got you into the Bureau's Wakening Room. Without it, there was no evidence left. The person you worked for was probably mixed in with really bad people, drug runners or who knows what. But the money laundering was his racket, something I became aware of on our side a few years ago from an old case file but there wasn't substantial proof. I couldn't move forward with my colleagues without evidence. You, however, figured out what and how he was doing this and stashed the information in the bottom drawer for safekeeping until your contact could find you, but it was too late. Then the unexpected happened... the military person who you've identified as someone from Limbo, finished the job before you could turn state's evidence to convict them."

"William," my voice trembled with fear and horror at the words I hadn't spoken, "I didn't tell anyone about evidence in a bottom drawer or a contact. Just who the hell are you?"

Chapter 20

Shoving from the wall, William left the room without a word, his jaw set rigid. Artemus and Mortimer closed the door behind him, leaving only the meager glowing light from the lantern to flicker from the middle of the table.

"Told ya he was quick," Mortimer said. "But let's see if he can keep up..." Bringing out a stack of ledgers from the corner in a box, he dumped them unceremoniously onto the table. "There ya go genius. Take a look."

"Not until you tell me why you know details about my death that I didn't share with anyone," I growled. Flo paced in the corner snapping her fingers in agitation as Artemus opened one of the books, worry chipping away each fingernail as she nipped at them.

"Looky here kid. The money that fool boss of yours laundered, is here in Limbo. You found it!" Artemus said pushing the book my way. As I thumbed through the first few pages, I remembered writing in it but not what I thought. "Your subconscious remembered what was in the original books. You've been transcribing your memory for days. Will knows people's ticks and habits, never play cards with the guy. Oi! When ya brought up the discrepancies and started locking the books away, he watched over you."

"Honey, you were reliving your final days," Flo said sympathy cooing as she sat next to me. "He was so worried for you, especially when you came to him in confidence. The numbers wouldn't match because they couldn't. They were numbers from the living world both from your time alive and now. We aren't supposed to have that type of currency in those amounts here. Our bank can't handle the transactions without setting off alerts to certain banks on the living side that we have no contracts with. Our bank shares the backside of another in the other world as a sort of neutral meeting ground and portal."

"The reason Will knows so much about your death is that he's been tracking every motion of every person and every little thing to do with you since just before you arrived. The Manager never takes a personal interest in anybody, not even Elvis. But you..." Artemus said waggling a finger, "you weren't supposed to be here. You were supposed to live to turn in the evidence and send your scumbag boss and his cronies to jail."

"But that no good rotten son of a, well, whatever you kids call'em these days," Mortimer said. "He had a guy on his payroll to run you over, do whatever it took to get you out of the picture. We know this because you wrote it down as a sidebar kinda scribble on one of the pages. Couldn't make out what it was until today when Will put two and two together. Just little weird doodles here and there. Look there - tires on a vehicle," he said pointing to an area with circles and lines in every direction connected by odd boxes. "They may not have meant anything to you when you were alive, but everything means something when you're dead. Believe me, you."

"Then Henry happened," Arty said shaking his head. "It devastated him. Crushed him to the core. He was trying to watch over everybody, but the more he focused on you, well..."

"He lost track and lost Henry as a result," I said, just realizing how terrible I'd been. "So the military guy is here with his buddies to do what? Why do Dejesh and Sonja want us out of the way so badly? Whatever they're doing, can't they just do it and leave us alone?"

"Isn't he cute?" Flo said, almost condescendingly. "Look sugar, he's been the only one keeping up with everything until you and Henry stumbled into that mess at the warehouse. Evey witnessed a military guy with Sonja kill Henry when he wouldn't give his key to them; snapped his neck like a dry twig. Problem was, poor thing was trying to get around more without it so he left the card with Evey. That's why they couldn't find it. The door was already open when they assumed she'd left on a food run so they shoved his body into the alcove and packed all those crates with coffee beans to hide his body and scent. When she didn't come back, they had to leave. They want her and the key to the door awful bad."

"But if the doors open, why not just go through? Do whatever it is and leave?"

"It's not dialed in to wherever they were going to disappear to," Arty said. "I suspect a place with no extradition and lots of pina coladas."

"I been here," Evey said crossing her arms. "I been good, gave Will cards and stayed put." Turning to her I thrummed my fingers across the table.

"But do you trust him?" I asked.

"You brain ice cream thick? You no listening?" Evey huffed rolling her eyes, throwing her hands exasperated into the air. "He suspected laundering but couldn't prove it. You come along and wham! In one day prove it. How come you no meet with Manager? You think 'bout that?" I hadn't considered it until she mentioned it. Now it stuck with me. The highlighted Friday note wasn't about a meeting with management, it was a meeting with my contact, the Manager - William. "You and nice boy Henry come help me. I'm no stupid. I know you two not lost. You come looking for answers to questions Henry had like others before you. No answers, just more questions." Shaking her head, Evey patted my hands in hers. "Wil not all knowing all sentient being. He just Will."

Resting my face in my hands I felt and probably looked the fool. "Gods I was such a prick to him. Wait, where'd he go off to? Those guys are still after him. He shouldn't be alone." Popping up from the bench my adrenaline kicked in. "I've gotta find him." Turning to Evey I hugged her tight, "Thanks for kicking my sensibilities' ass. I needed it."

"Anytime you need a swift kick, you come to Evey. I kick you, no problem," she said grinning ear to ear.

"I'm not sure how to take that but, thanks." Turning to leave, Evey grabbed me by the arm, jerking me to the floor.

"Quiet. Someone here." Blowing out the light, Mortimer crouched next to the door.

"Hello, anybody here?" came the echo of Dejesh's voice in the main entryway. "Just wanna talk." Bumping up next to me in the dark, Flo mussed her hair and licked her palm, running it over her face vigorously. Then pulled her clothing askew on her shoulders and hips.

"Wait here, and not a noise," she whispered, cracking open the door. "Cripes! What the hell time is it?" she yawned shuffling her feet.

"Sorry to wake you but," Sonja asked then paused, waving her hand through the dusty air, "Jeez, do you sleep here too?"

"What?" Flo snapped, "I can't always make it home. The coffins can be comfy when they need to be." Exaggerating a yawn she arched, popping her back. "What can I do ya fer?"

"We have reason to believe our client, Randy, came here. We just want to give him the good news," the words were there but Sonja's conviction was flat and coldly missing. "His file's ready to sign off on, tonight. Isn't that great?"

"Yeah great. Morty, Arty, get yer keesters in here. Got

company," she yelled. Following her lead, the men did as she'd done and rumpled their clothes and ran a spit-laden hand through their hair.

"What, what, what?" Arty sneezed shuffling up next to her. "Got a body or what?"

"Kids is looking for Randy. Wants him to sign off, now," she huffed yawning again.

"Great news, just great," Mortimer replied in a drone almost uncaring way. "Now can we get some sleep?"

"So, you haven't seen him?" Dejesh asked, peering down the aisle. "I'm surprised you didn't tell him I'd been here that first day."

"Didn't matter. You found the back door," Morty growled, "now you can find the front one. Don't let it hit your arse on the way out."

"Yeah, yeah he was by here earlier. Dropped off some cosmetics for us. What a nice guy," Arty said grinning and squinting. "Unlike some people who won't let the dead sleep."

"Sorry to bother you," Dejesh said apologetically, backing away.

"You sure he isn't still here?" Sonja asked, nosing her way around the front crates of the dusty room.

"Look here li'l lady, I don't know you or why you're still here after rudely waking us but I'm inclined to kick your lily white rump on principal alone. Randy left hours ago. Maybe he went home and is asleep like some of us would like to be," Flo said, pushing up her sleeves. Man, she needs an award too. Instead of Daytime Drama, she could be crowned Night Time Drama Queen with no contenders.

"Just making sure," Sonja said, her hands coming up passively as she noticed a few sharp instruments nearby now appearing in their hands. "If you see him, let us know. It's important."

"Sure, if we see'em through the back of our eyelids," Arty snorted, waving one hand dismissively. "I'm going back to bed."

Before he made it back to the room, the door to the shop closed and latched behind Flo. "Oh, good lord I thought I was gonna have to scrap that scrawny suit," she whispered coming in behind Mortimer. "Place is locked up, we'll have to leave through the back. Honey, I'm sorry but you'll have to leave your card here. Wil was right, they'll track you with it." Pulling it from my pocket I laid it on the table, staring down at the blank surface.

"Show me where William is located," I spoke into it. In seconds the map of the city showed a copper line from Props to William's office. "Good enough. You guys were, how should I put this...better than late night tv," I said hugging Flo. "Whatever you're doing, be careful, stick together. Don't get caught. I'd die another death if I thought you guys, well..."

"We know sugar," Flo said, her smile almost Cheshire in the near darkness, it wasn't much of a stretch to believe she'd once been a thief. "Take care and I guess I shouldn't say see ya on the other side, you know what I mean." Giving Evey a last hug and handshakes to Arty and Mortimer, I followed them out the back door of the complex. Splitting up the four made their way eerily quiet to the next building, then disappeared into the shadows.

Chapter 21

My feet carried me several paces behind, and hopefully out of sight, of Sonja and Dejesh as they meandered down Shirley toward Cragston, flicking their keycards between their fingers. Occasionally attempting to look casually over their shoulders, I got the feeling they knew they were being watched.

Once they turned onto Cragston, they strolled past my office and another block past the bank where I took a chance and backtracked to the office door and slid inside. Shutting and locking it still didn't feel safe enough. As they said before, they were still FBI agents with the instincts they'd always carry.

Without the constant hum of white noise from the computers and lights, the place emanated a deafening quiet. Step by step, I backed slowly away from the doors, hearing my feet, too loudly, drag across the carpet, the only noise in the room. Every second spent in anticipation, was finally rewarded with two shadows approaching then pausing only a few feet away but unattached to its owners. Beads of sweat accumulated, running down my back in the stagnant darkness as my heart raced. Freezing in place I waited for the two shadows to merge with their physical owners who I could only assume were Sonja and Dejesh. A split second later I was being dragged unwillingly backward with a hand firmly clamped over my mouth and an arm across my chest.

"Shush," Vanessa whispered taking her hands away. "William's waiting for us." Nodding, I could only swallow relief against the dryness in my throat. Following her closely we made our way down the hall to his office where, once inside, William shut the door and pushed a button hidden beneath his desk. The electricity vibrated the air as a two-inch thick plate glass reinforced door slid and locked into place.

The only light illuminating the room emanating from the green-shaded banker's lamp on the corner. Behind his desk, William sat with his fingers tapping the surface. "Mind telling me what you were doing out there?" he growled.

"Me?" Not my best comeback but hey, I'm working on shot nerves and no food here. "Why'd you run off like that?"

"To protect you," he said blandly not looking up at me. "I'll ask again, what were you doing out there with them?"

"I wasn't with them, I was trying to get to you," I explained. "They traced my card to Props." That got him to look up. "Don't worry, they're all right. They got rid of them." Beside me Vanessa's hands went to her face as she sighed in relief, visibly shaking as if she wanted to cry or scream or both. Only now did I realize how she'd been able to sneak up behind me, she was barefoot, showing burn marks up to her ankles and crooked toes, her shoes sharing a chair with a large purse nearby.

Pushing from his chair William leaned on his desk, looking me in the eyes, "You could've been killed if they saw you," he ground out. "Don't ever take a chance like that again." Breaking eye contact I shrugged. "I mean it. I won't have you ending up like Henry."

"I know, I got it," I said, the guilt building in my shoulders weighing them down. "You're not omnipotent, you're just Will."

"What?" he asked, the confusion scrunching his face.

"Never mind, been hanging around Evey too long," I said. Quirking my head toward Vanessa, William seemed to get what I wasn't verbally asking.

"She's fine. She'll be staying here for the foreseeable future," he said waving the question off.

"Vanessa's been supporting you from the beginning and I suspect your caseworkers may be aware of this."

"You mean like keeping my desk buried beneath work?" I snorted derisively.

"No silly," Vanessa said rolling her eyes. "I've been supplying you with the monthly and back reports the agents have been turning in so you could 'balance' them. We knew they were falsified, just - I don't know what I'm looking for and neither does William. You, however..."

"I, however, am a numbers guy, just say it." It doesn't

even phase me they're using my natural talents to secretly investigate these clowns, but what bugs me is they didn't even ask. "So now what? They get away with murder and laundering? We can't leave this room without them knowing or finding us. We can't fight the military - they're armed to the teeth and outnumber us. And quite frankly, sooner or later, they're gonna come gunning for all of us and that plate glass won't hold them off." That sounded more desperate than I wanted but the truth will out. I'm waiting for that ye of li'l faith thing he does to come up with a brilliant plan. Any second now...

"You're right, we can't fight them. We don't have reinforcements to call on, we're just seven people; they're...I don't know how many, too many." Rubbing his chin worriedly with one hand, I watched the wheels behind his eyes calculate and turn, "We're screwed." Seeing William deflate into his chair with his head hung in his hands hurt to the core. He's run this place for years making sure everyone was protected, helped and safe. Now, all the agents have to do is rush us and we're all deader than dead - permanently.

"What was your plan?" I asked.

"Doesn't matter," he said agitated, his eyes darting around the room with Vanessa standing behind him squeezing his shoulders. Swallowing hard his hand patted one of hers, steadying it.

"You remember who to go to?" he asked as she nodded vigorously, his eyes now sternly capturing mine.

"Yeah, I do," her voice quaked. "I don't want you to do this. There's gotta be another way," she sobbed softly.

"Vanessa, I'm counting on you," he said solemnly, not taking his eyes away.

Breathing deeply, she backed away, picking up her purse and moving behind me to my right. As I turned my attention back to William to put my two cents worth in, I barely got my mouth open when I caught one last sight of her swinging hard, the lamp connecting with the back of my head sending me into unconsciousness.

When on earth was it ever a good idea not to listen to wise adages from old movies? Never go to a haunted cemetery alone at night in high heels - you're destined to trip in the dark and be a victim. Never let yourself be invited to a creepy mansion in the middle of nowhere without at least fifteen armed ex-military people with you - otherwise, you're asking for a dismemberment from some maniac with a machete. And most of all, never trust the blond lady in a spy movie, she's there to knock you out and keep you from derailing the bad guy's plans - but in my case, I realize she did it to keep me from harm's way. Still, hurts like a son of a bitch but, not as much as being on this side of a bulletproof room. Nope, like William said, this shit ends now! Pulling myself up from the floor with a well-deserved moan, I checked the back of my head. It's still intact but aching like, well frankly, like I've been hit with a lamp.

The stillness surrounding me isn't helping my nerves. Going from almost no lighting in a relatively safe environment with people I care about to unadulterated creepy desolate darkness is about all I can take.

Moving lethargically I reached for the button beneath his desk and released the bulletproof door. Moments earlier I was certain of my intentions, eager to find them and help in any way I can. Now, the sound of the lock snapping open, the glass slowly sliding back, grumbling in its tracks, stripping away the only thing that's standing between me staying safe and the uncertain world of an undead FBI hunting party searching for us has a certain air of what the Hell am I doing to it.

Chapter 22

How do you know when to give up or when to give in? You don't until it happens. One moment I'm thinking - I'm dreaming, this is all a weird hallucination brought on by cold leftovers and alcohol, the next I'm wishing it *had* been a dream. For some odd reason, I found myself hunched over in the dark sneaking around an empty office searching frantically for anything: a gun, knife, bulletproof vest, Vanessa, and William. What I found was my instincts going straight for the bottom left drawer of my desk which had been forced open and the journals removed.

Unintentionally slamming the drawer the pitch echoed all around, jamming my already fragile anxiety state up to another level I never thought possible; until I heard a terrifying familiar rumble coming up the street.

Scurrying to get a peek out the front doors from behind the safety of the break room wall, my heart skipped a beat. The full moon illuminated the streets brightly and white washed scenery eerily with its intensity. Everything literally glowing, devouring the shadows and darkness, anything that could shelter a person from view. Except for the humvee truck creeping by being driven by a person in fatigue camouflage wearing a gas mask, escorted by none other than Dejesh and Sonja and two unknown caseworkers in identical suits.

Ducking back quickly I hugged the only shadow against the wall, a temporary safe place away from the beams from flashlights cutting through the shroud of darkness into the room, inches from where I'm standing. The glass doors being brutally rattled almost to the breaking point before they moved on, leaving me to nearly wet myself. Unwilling to move I waited in the deafening quiet until it hit me, I know this office better than anyone. Scurrying around the corners and edges of desks and cubicles in the darkness, I didn't need to see. I practically spent years subconsciously mapping every centimeter in the living world, just like I had done with the journals, stowing the information away.

The northeast corner of the building has a back door secured with an alarm but having been who I was growing up, I wasn't much of a 'bend' or 'break the rules' kind of person; until these jerks killed Henry and put everyone in harm's way, and now I find myself sliding an envelope along the top of the door to find the triggering mechanism.

Cautiously rounding the outside of the building, his shadow pulled to the wall, out of sight of the truck and its entourage pulling into the street. As it approached his form disappeared onto Cragston, making his way to the bank. From three streets down on Fairbanks where I'd normally turn to go home, a well-tailored suit appeared. Standing in the middle, his jacket loosened with his hands in his pockets, waiting patiently. The truck turned the corner onto Cragston, making another pass by work before the agents pointed to the figure. In the blink of an eye, the well-dressed man fled to the cross streets, the truck speeding up but unable to make the corners as quickly. Taking my queue I turned the door knob and walked through.

The bank was a typical layout and easy to get around. In the back, true to Vanessa's words, was a door I had just come through that resembled the one in the warehouse, and lit. Pulling it open, the other side mirrored our world with the same desks, lamps, counters, and lollipops at each station. What was different, however, wasn't just the steady blue light I'd stepped from but the blond now staring at me from the center of a group of people in suits and elegant personalized gas mask apparatus she'd been in conversation with moments ago.

"Excuse me, please," Vanessa said, smiling in a friendly business manner, which meant fake and pissed as she approached me. "Cripes!" she vented under her breath. "What the living hell are you doing here? You were supposed to stay where we could protect you."

Ignoring her I gestured, "And who might these people be?" Tugging my arm she pulled me aside.

"These people run this and many other banks and businesses like the FBI. See the old short guy with the glasses who looks like every other person's grandpa? That's the Director of National Intelligence," she said.

"And he just happens to be here at whatever this ungodly hour is?" I asked keeping my voice low.

"He's here because William purposely tripped an

alarm earlier tonight to warrant them being summoned here. It was all pre-planned to catch the thieves and culprits but with everything that's been going on, the time table's been moved up." Nervously tapping her foot she blinked hard once.

Well, shit. There goes Rules 16 and 4, right out the proverbial window. Here we stood on this side of the gateway mingling with the living and I'm pretty sure the portal was wide open and was going to stay that way.

"Speaking of - where is he?" she asked, looking back over my shoulder.

"William," I responded, "was last seen giving the agents a merry chase down Fairbanks and headed towards the warehouse, I think."

"Oh my gods no," Vanessa said grabbing the arms of the shirt. "If they catch him..."

"They won't." I couldn't tell if I was lying or just trying to convince the both of us he was that good. "He's resourceful. But whatever your plan is, it needs to happen now."

"I need your help. We have to convince these codgers that the books are real, the danger is real, and military really is in Limbo," she said taking a deep breath. "It's one in the morning and they're cranky, so keep it short." Wringing her hands she turned her attention back to them, addressing them as one. "Gentlemen and lady, this is my colleague, Randy. He's been deciphering the ledgers and is your witness to the money laundering events, and more. Tell them." Giving me a rough nudge I stood motionless, mouth gaped open. Of the eleven people standing before me, only one caught my attention and for once it wasn't the woman.

"Well, he's informative. I could have gotten this much from my dog at home," the Director's snarky comment began souring my disposition as he checked his watch for the fourth time. Obviously he had somewhere important to be, like somewhere other than here.

"I'm not sure where to begin or what you need to convince you," I said as a pudgy man adjusting his peacoat shuffled to the back.

"Young man, this meeting hinges on Mr. Thorpe's presence. If you can't produce him, we can't help you," said a whiny weasel of a man off to my right who obviously was there to conclude everything as quick as possible. His job was to move things along and be the Closer - the person you go to when you can't win or close a deal, they force it or bring it to a conclusion amicable for the parties. This guy was a bureaucratic blight on society, plain and simple. But he worked for someone else. Someone in the back.

"Is that so?" I asked milling through the group, nudging my shoulders to theirs. "The way I see it, whoever set this up with Will needs to call in the cavalry, now." Stepping up to the man in the back, his collar flips up, obscuring part of his face. "You may need the police, FBI, some military and when I'm done with you - an ambulance," I said poking him in the chest. "I know you. I know what you did. I remember everything now." The mild headache pulsing between my ears was nothing compared to the rage building in my bones. "Where is he?"

"I don't know what you're talking about," the man in the peacoat said, tugging at the collar again. "And I certainly don't know you."

"You like playing games? Games with other people's time, jobs, money...lives?" I asked circling him in small measured steps. "Devin, Derick, Dan..." Grinning, he huffed heavily, shoving his hands in his coat pockets.

"You have no idea who you're talking to, do you?"

"David. David...Cap, Capra...Cappela," my fingers snapped with the words falling into place.

"You were my supervisor. You're the one who had me running errands to the laundry facilities every Tuesday. Pickups and drop-offs to the bank on Thursdays. Things I thought, at the time were innocuous. Until I dropped the laundry getting out of the company car and nearly half a million dollars rained to the ground at my feet." Shifting his eyes, David swallowed nervously, adjusting his footing. "You made sure you stood behind a bulletproof door, calmly looking at your watch just as a truck came crashing through the wall at the very moment I was at my desk. You had me killed and didn't bat an eyelash."

"You're looney." Looking to his constituents, David attempted a smile, forcing the edges of his mouth upward. "If half of what I hear is true, then you're dead and your memory can't be trusted. Every word you spoke is rubbish and even if I looked at my watch, everyone looks at their watch. It means nothing. You're grasping and I can understand why you would."

Condescending tones in place -check, placation to the ego - check, playing the game - check. Here we go. "After all, if I were in your shoes I'd want justice of some sort. I'd imagine all kinds of things. I sympathize, really, but just because I want something to be true doesn't mean it is. A word of advice - you should really learn to let go of this." Behind me the group involuntarily had pushed to the walls close together, some shaking their heads as they pulled out their phones, eyeing me skeptically.

"Vanessa, please distribute the journals to the others." On my request, she placed them in their hands, letting them flip through while on hold.

"Rubbish," David smirked, pointing to the journals as they read. "You can't believe any of this. Those could very well have been faked." Turning the pages, several people had already made up their minds. And by their looks, David was winning. As soon as the Director had a journal in his hands, he shut the book and passed it along without looking. "See? Even he doesn't believe any of this. Look at them, none of them do."

Adjusting his glasses the Director sighed, laying a finger to the mic he had worn hidden in his ear, "Do it." In moments the front of the bank doors to the living world slammed back as a group of police entered with their hands on their holstered weapons. Turning to me the Director asks,

"Can you prove any of these allegations?" Nodding I reached into my pocket and pulled out a small key, then handed it over to him.

"This opens the bottom left drawer to my old desk. In it, you'll find six ledgers I kept on transactions dating back five years. I can also prove he had me killed," I said, my chest tightening at the memory. "The man driving the truck that came through the wall was one of the same military people that have been using Limbo to store their stolen and laundered goods. He's in a truck right now hunting William with ex-FBI agents Sonja and Dejesh." It was supposed to be a weight lifted, to unburden myself. But right now it feels like heavy boulders being laid on top of me one by one, crushing me beneath an invisible weight. The look in their eyes telling me I still had no solid evidence, and the cops were here not to arrest David, but me.

Chapter 23

It's important to know the rules of any game you play. Like now, for instance, the rules are in David's favor, no duh. He's been at this a lot longer than I have. In hindsight, maybe I tipped my only card by telling him where the evidence is located. Maybe I should have snuck back into the living world and recovered the books first. Maybe I should have been the one to lead the chase and have William where he needed to be, in this impromptu meeting. Maybe I should have had a better plan than off the cuff but let's face it, honestly, I never thought I'd be in my shoes right now. Let's face it, I suck at games that require anticipation and strategy. David probably knows this and is counting on my lack of forethought. Man, he's cocky. He probably set this whole thing up from the beginning. And he's still living behind that bulletproof glass. Untouchable. But not irreproachable.

Turning to Vanessa I shot a quick wide-eyed look to the weasel, then flicked my head toward the door. "You want me, come-n get me. Now!" I yelled as she grabbed one arm and I the other, dragging David's Closer out the door into Limbo with us.

"Great," she said as we entered Cragston. "Now what?"

"Haven't gotten that far," I replied.

"What? I thought you had a plan or something?" she

whined.

"No, that was you and William and it seems to have gone cockeyed at the moment. I'm just improvising," I said hoping for a miracle, my head on a swivel at the sound of David's voice.

"And where do you think you're going with him? He doesn't know anything and doesn't belong here. None of us do, so release him and come along quietly," he said smugly, the police now joining him. "No one has to get hurt."

"You're right," I said. "No one did. I realize I can't stop you in the living world, but I can do something about it here." The unmistakable sound of a small golf cart whizzing around Shirley
onto Cragston brought all our attention around.

"Taxi?" Evey said pulling up a few feet away. Without waiting, Vanessa and I had the Closer in the back with us, and surprisingly, the Director took the seat up front.

"Warehouse, Evey. You know which one," Vanessa said elbowing the squirming Closer into sitting still.

Rounding the bend from behind my apartments, the Director seemed to take in the scenery much the way, with a frown. Calmly scrutinizing the gates up ahead he gave her a forward signal, "Ram it." Without letting up, she did just that, and the gates popped open with a jolt.

Trucks lined up in front of the dock where military personnel handed box after box in a human chain loading them, their commanding officer barking orders to move faster. In the middle of all the hustle stood a group of caseworkers arguing graphically among themselves with Sonja leading their fiery discussion. Except for Dejesh, who stood off to the left side holding a gun pointed at William, kneeling and bound.

Hopping from the cart the Director didn't wait for it to stop. "Cease and desist all activity," he commanded angrily. Several people looked to one another but did not stop as their commander walked to the edge of the dock, addressing him.

"You have no jurisdiction here Director," he sneered, the mask muffling his voice only a little.

"And in a few minutes, we'll disappear off your grid, and you'll have no proof we ever even existed." Sneering and signaling his men to wrap it up, he threw his hand forward toward the end of the city block. Deep rumbling vibrated the area as the drivers turned the engines, the lead truck rolling forward. Pushing our shoulders, we stood, dragging the Closer with us as Evelyn floored the pedal, swinging out front to line up with the lead driver. A young man with a chip on his shoulder versus an older pissed off Asian lady with nothing to lose, it was a destined battle he lost as soon as she crashed her cart into the front grill, screaming unintelligible remarks the whole time. I would have laughed at her had it not been for the deathly quiet that came soon after the crunching of his tires and squealing of metal meeting metal ended.

Beside me, Vanessa's breath sucked in harsh at the sight. Taking the opportunity, the Closer jerked his arms, squirming to get away. But her vice grip only yanked harder keeping him locked firmly between us, "Move again and that'll be you under his tires next," she warned.

"I'm not afraid of you," he spat.

"You should be. My ex was a mob boss. I know how to inflict pain, and make it last an eternity," she purred dangerously next to his ear, gaining his placation.

Throwing his hands up before him, the Director pleaded, "You're right. If I let you go, no one else has to get hurt." His attention now settling on Dejesh. "I read the files on you and your group here. Took a bullet for your partner during a drug cartel bust. Nothing rings truer than the loyalty of someone who would do that for you. But the person you protected was also under internal investigation for acts of perjury, misconduct, falsifying documents, and attempted murder of a fellow agent."

"They couldn't prove any of that," Dejesh balked, the gun waving in his hand. "None of that was true," he said, his eyes darting between William and Sonja. Long moments of silence stretched as her hand slowly inched toward her holster. "You were my partner. I died for you." The sorrow and anger in his face twitching the cheek muscles.

"Dejesh, you were a fine agent once. You can walk away from this, just put the gun down," the Director said, putting one foot in front of the other toward Sonja, reaching the edge of the dock.

Taking a deep breath, Dejesh wavered his gun momentarily, "I can't just walk away, can I?" A split second later, the silence was shattered by a sudden thunderous eruption, akin to the deep sound of fireworks exploding high in the air, causing us all to flinch and leaving a hole through his neck and Sonja collapsing to the ground holding her shoulder in pain. Spinning in place with our ears still ringing we looked on as the barrel of David's gun smoldered from the end.

"Unless you wish to share his fate, you'll back away Director," David said waving him to move. Doing as he was told, the Director skirted his way along the edge of the group of agents now huddling next to the wall.

It was obvious the plan had been derailed long ago and been progressively getting worse; we were just floundering moment to moment hoping for a miracle or some divine intervention, anything to sway in our favor. But unlike the others, I don't believe in such things. I also know I'm not a hero but damn it, I had to do something, "David, make a trade." My insides shaking I wanna throw up. To be in the presence of the person who carries out cold blooded murder is nerve wracking. Now what? Think. Think! "This guy for William. The Director can't prove anything. Even if he brought any of this up to the outside world they'd have him in a straight jacket in minutes." A non-committal shrug, better than a bullet I suppose. Tugging the Closer with me, Vanessa let go. "He can't do anything to you. None of us can leave, and if we did we'd have nothing to say." Before I knew it I was handing over the only leverage we have to the Director, who clamped onto his arm tight. "Give us William, let us go, and you guys can be on your merry way. No harm, no foul, everybody wins." By now my feet carried me subconsciously up the stairs onto the dock where Sonja had been taken off to the side by the other agents. Unbinding William's wrists, I helped him stand; his thanks being whispered beneath his breath. "These people aren't your problem, they're William's. He'll deal with the caseworkers here, that includes Sonja. The military is off the grid. You heard them, they're planning on disappearing, never to be heard from again," I said, watching the military leader back away. "You win," I exhaled a long deep shaky breath, "just let us go and this all goes away."

I couldn't tell where all the sighs of relief came from but when he lowered his gun, they seemed to come from everyone. Jerking his arm away, the Closer sneered victory, wiping down the sleeves of his coat arrogantly as if dusting off an irritant.

"Randy," David said, the wheels turning visibly behind his calculating eyes, coming to a conclusion, "you've made quite the astute point, and once again, you're right. Then again, you're always right." Raising the gun, his eyes met mine and there was no color. His pupils had dilated fully open, bringing chills to my spine and the hair on my arms to stand upright. "I could simply - leave everyone here."

Chapter 24

Allow me to introduce one of my own rules - if your closest friend takes a bullet for you, you're probably entitled to beat the ever living crap outta the guy who did it. I wasn't alone in this new rule though. Somewhere in the mix of bloodied fists flying and bodies falling from gunfire was my snapped sanity. Beneath me lay David's remains as the Director gods only knew who else struggled to pull me from him. All I knew was he was dead and I was still pounding my fists into his face from uncontrollable rage and tears. I do know it happened soon after he began firing and killed Sonja, then took out his Closer at close range, who never saw it coming. Poor bastard. Then it was my turn. I was lined up in his sights, unable to move and transfixed on the barrel swinging my way. That's when the next bullet found William's chest instead of mine, and he'd jumped between us to save me.

Honestly, the parade on foot of law enforcement couldn't have arrived at a better time being led by Arty, Morty and Flo. Smoke continued to waft in spirals around us from smoke grenades the military obviously thought would be a good idea to use to cover their would-be escape, only they never made it out of the courtyard or to the front gate. Something about flat tires and some Asian woman savagely wielding a knife slitting them and anyone who tried to run.

Shell casings littered the place, clinking beneath boots as our cavalry of friends in the real FBI and a large band of military personnel began the process of mopping up the mess and arresting the remaining living and confiscating the evidence.

Ignoring me, the police scooped up David's body and carried it off on a litter somewhere I wasn't paying attention to because on the dock my mind raced back to where William lay now being cradled by a weeping and shaken Vanessa. The way she tenderly stroked back the hair from his face you'd swear she had feelings for him. With Flo by her side, I know she'll do everything in her power for them.

As for my own experiences inside of a few short weeks, it has me reevaluating the whole introvert thing. I think I just wasn't around the right people or in the right place to fit in. Sure it sucks for me to have died to find out where I belong but there's something comforting knowing I eventually found it. But I know deep down inside, if I'd been able to meet these people on the living side, I know we'd have been friends. I would have had a life instead of late night television. We would have hung out at the local tavern and maybe I would have been their liaison. I just can't use the phrase better late than never, especially when I didn't really give the living side a fair try.

"Mind if I join you?" I'll never get tired of hearing William pull up a barstool and wanna knock back a few drinks with me. Waving a hand to the empty seat, he leaned across the counter. Pulling the half empty bottle of bourbon from the back of the bar, judging it to be worthy with a wry smirk, he twists open the top and pours a two finger serving into the tumbler and sits next to me, leaving the bottle between us.   "Still breathing," he said, tossing back half his drink. Topping it off, he rolls it between his palms in thought, "thanks to you."

"It was all Props brother," I said stealing a shot from his bottle. "They were incredible." Shaking my head, I peered down into my glass, "I was never so scared in all my life. You're the one I should be thanking. You literally took a bullet for me."

"I couldn't let him shoot you in cold blood," he shrugged empathetically. "This was my fault, I want you to know that, and I own it."

"Cripes Will, you're not to blame," I huffed shaking my empty glass. "Shut up and fill this." Grinning sadly he tipped the bottle until I waved him to stop a finger width from the top. "You had a solid plan and things went zippy zappy. It happens. The important thing is that we all worked together, sorta, and survived. Justice was served," I replied smirking."I do have one question though."

"Shoot, metaphorically of course," he grinned.

"What's the deal with the masks? Seriously, it's creepy and reminds me of an old World War 1 movie where someone sets off a toxic bomb and everyone has to wear these filters to breathe."

"You're not far from the truth," he replied. "Point

blank? The dead stink," he shrugged. "We're stuck in a type of paused state of decay. We can't smell each other but to the living, we smell worse than three-year-old dirty gym socks wrapped around decaying fish laying in the sun or something. The Director once told me after we first met that I smelled like Chicago garbage on a summer day. I took it as a compliment."

"That's absolutely disgusting," I said nudging him playfully. "So that's why they used the coffee beans, to literally hide Henry's stench and the people who were helping them in Limbo."

"Yup," he said turning in his seat. "That reminds me, I need to have a little chat with Evelyn one of these days."

"The cart was mangled, I saw it. How did she survive?" I asked but all he would do was shake his head with a weary half grin.

"Who knows with her?" he shrugged. "All she'd tell me was that it was some sort of ancient ninja thing then she patted my hand like I was five. I never know if she's joking or telling the truth."

Behind us the doors to the bar swings open and the familiar cheerleader Bronx sound of Vanessa's exuberant voice chimes with that of Flo, Arty, Evey and Morty as they enter. Grabbing bar stools of their own they help themselves to the liquor on the shelves and cold beer on tap. The first round clinked salutes to Henry whose body Props had recovered that night and buried promptly in a plot next to Elvis in the Bureau's garden out back.

Saluting Vanessa, I left my place to come stand behind her. Leaning in, I pretended to reach for another bottle of Scotch from behind the bar, "I'll get on your files tomorrow, promise." Turning towards me she laid a sweet soft kiss on my cheek.

"That won't be necessary," she whispered, leaving her seat to go sit next to William on my abandoned stool.

I didn't have the heart to tell her I'd not only found her file but some of William's too. It was something she'd said earlier, something about being an ex drug mafia boss's wife. It got me to thinking about case files that were still open so I sort of snuck into William's office and kind of borrowed a few of his personal files he had locked up. Surprisingly, Vanessa's file was directly tied to William's.

Somehow, she'd managed to find out about a double cross sting operation her ex husband was conducting on the night of William's murder. As it happened, they didn't have cell phones back in 1969. The file I came across in William's office was one of his own personal files. An open case he never got to close. Husband. Father. Son. And Chief FBI Investigator. Friend and something of a hero to a confidant. He was all of those things. An interesting name had been redacted nearly a hundred times in his file. But with a little help from Props I was able to differentiate between the two inks and pull them apart gently, leaving the faint image of Vanessa's name behind. She wanted out of an abusive marriage - he helped her get that. She wanted a new life - he gave her a new identity.

She wanted to take her slime ball ex husband down for money laundering - but she wasn't able to get to William in time to warn him about the ambush. She found out that fateful night William had been murdered. She'd intended to go to the cops with what evidence she had, but her ex had made sure she suffered in a fire. Sadly, William never knew she was killed and left to burn in her ex's office, along with the amassed evidence. So yes, she arrived in limbo shortly after William. Yes, I suspect, she remembered most of what happened and carried a heavy burden on her thin shoulders.

I guess it's why she wanted to leave so badly. She couldn't stand being around someone she liked and felt she'd somehow betrayed, and ultimately felt responsible for their death, even though she wasn't. Although I have to say, William may not have remembered what happened or her involvement since she wasn't on his mind when he died. Maybe that's why she remembered him so vividly? Maybe he was her last thoughts. And maybe that's why he remembered his son so vividly.

After a few moments, everyone fell into more light-hearted conversations related to work and the reconstruction of Limbo. Apparently, the FBI and police are donating a lot of paint and fresh sod to be installed on the orders of the Director who thinks we need a little color in our lives; can't really blame him. As for William and Vanessa's files, I'm keeping it to myself — for now.. I'll have plenty of time to get all the details nailed down before I present my findings to them both.

And then there's Rule No. 94 - the written law applies to all.

It goes without saying that even the law will find its way to you in the afterlife, so don't go screwing things up living. Not everyone gets the second chance that Flo did. But I guess some people can't help themselves. It didn't work out for poor Henry even though it wasn't his fault. His second chance was stolen from him when he was murdered. And then there's the King. Elvis had everything going for him and in the end, his ego for food did him in a second time. I get it, some things can't be helped. They're out of our control. But, if you follow those rules, those horribly written, government reading, zombie bland manual, gods awful boring rules – you have a chance to do things better. To do things right. Maybe even make amends, like Vanessa and William. I have a feeling those two have a steep history together and Limbo is likely the only place they'll find peace and friendship.

And I'm adding a new rule when I rewrite this damn manual, and make no mistake, I *am* rewriting it: things rarely go as planned, but if given the chance, they might just work out anyway. Like it did for Flo, Morty, Art, William, Vanessa, and to a begrudging extent – me.

I didn't sign off on my file even though I have all the I's dotted the T's crossed and every detail of my own murder figured out and the culprit brought to justice. It seems this group may need to keep me around a while longer. Apparently I'm just enough of a geek to get some of the computers up and running and they'll need someone who knows the system to input all that data.

Besides, how would it look if I squelched on a promise? Vanessa needs closure and deserves the full story. So does poor William, though I suspect Vanessa will have to come clean with what she remembers one of these days. So, I just put in the paperwork for an extended stay in Limbo, no use trying to go somewhere that might just end up a bright light to nowhere and end my existence all together.

There were no angelic sounds or halos or magical doors promising a better world or graceful life beyond. All I know is there is a bar I share with my extended family of the undead – with no grand expectations, no pressure to find a way out, and nothing but time on our hands to help whoever else may come through the Bureau's Awakening doors - the way it should be.

More about the author can be found on
https://aralynblog.wordpress.com/

Stop by to check out the newest editions to her writing, and latest adventures in foodies and rv'ing.

A quick excerpt from her bio page:

For me, I read and created drawings because quite frankly it was fun. I loved reading! Still do. And when you're a kid with no where to go, not much else to do, and living in the middle of "meh"ville, you find ways to entertain yourself. And before you ask, no. The neighborhood kids were always in trouble and almost always grounded so there wasn't really a friend to go hang out with or play ball with, or even go fishing with.

My second love is a dead even passion for first place next to reading/writing -- roller skating. Hey! Don't laugh.

When we FINALLY moved from the sticks to the bigger sticks with less snakes, I ended up with a nice pair of cheap roller skates and fell deeply in love with them. I wore those suckers everywhere! Yes, I wore them out quickly. No, I didn't get another pair until I was thirteen. THAT pair lasted me over thirty years and worth every penny! I am, in fact, a rink rat. (All-night skating, suicide drinks (a soda with every flavor soda in it), good music, good friends, and great times.)

... All those times a person picks up a book and flips through it, they never realize how much effort and passion went into every syllable, every word, every page. Every time that author spent countless hours putting everything onto paper then editing the crap out of it so it makes sense. Then revision after revision after another fifteen revisions and waffling between what they need to have the story move forward and that one line or sentence they love and want to keep because it felt good to write. "I can't just ditch that! Whadda ya mean it doesn't make sense? I'll rewrite the whole damn book to make that one line make sense. You'll see!" Oh yeah. Writers are like that. Our work isn't always about how much we get out of it but how much we put into it. It's our blood, sweat, tears, hopes, fears, joys, elation of winning, heartache of losing, creation of worlds, people, fantastic creatures, perilous journeys, relationships that sometimes work and other times fail.

It's all us.

45754736R00138

Made in the USA
Columbia, SC
22 December 2018